KV-033-198

THE SURGEON'S PREGNANCY SURPRISE

BY
LAURA MacDONALD

MILLS & BOON®

First published in Great Britain 2006
Harlequin Mills & Boon Limited,
Eton House, 18-24 Paradise Road, Richmond, Surrey TW9 1SR

© Laura MacDonald 2006

ISBN 0 263 19117 6

Set in Times Roman 10½ on 12½ pt.
07-0106-48771

Printed and bound in Great Britain
by Antony Rowe Ltd, Chippenham, Wiltshire

CHAPTER ONE

THE bride and groom emerged from the church and the snow, which had been threatening all day, gently began to fall, a magical alternative to confetti. For Chrissie, as she watched her friend Caitlin look up into the face of her new husband Michael O'Reagan, it was the most romantic scene she had ever witnessed. Not that Chrissie herself was much into romance these days—not since her last relationship had ended a year before, leaving her feeling bruised, betrayed and utterly devastated—but she wouldn't let that cloud the joy she felt for Caitlin. When Caitlin had asked her if she would attend her wedding in Ireland she had happily accepted, in spite of the fact that it was in the middle of a particularly cold winter. Several of the staff of the Eleanor James Memorial Hospital in Sussex had made the trip across the Irish Sea to see their two colleagues, who had been childhood sweethearts, exchange their wedding vows.

'Isn't it just a picture she's looking?' exclaimed a woman standing near Chrissie.

'It is indeed,' Chrissie agreed, laughing as she brushed away a large snowflake from her mouth.

'I've known the pair of them since they were babes,' the

woman went on, a rapt expression on her face in spite of the cold. 'We always knew they would wed.'

'So did we.' Chrissie nodded and at that the woman half turned to cast her a curious glance. 'So is it a nurse you are, at the same hospital?' she asked.

'Well, I work at the same hospital, certainly, but I'm a doctor.'

'A doctor, you say?' The woman eyed her speculatively. 'So it's more Michael you're working with?'

'Not really.' Chrissie smiled and pulled the fur-trimmed collar of her coat more snugly around her. 'Michael works in another department—he's a registrar on orthopaedics.'

'That's bones, isn't it?'

'Yes.' Chrissie nodded again. 'But Caitlin and I work on the surgical unit.'

The woman digested this particular piece of information in silence, then moved away, apparently determined to throw her confetti in spite of the conditions. Her place was almost immediately taken by Alison Spicer, another of Caitlin's friends who worked on the surgical unit at Ellie's (as it was affectionately known by staff and patients alike) who had travelled from England for the occasion.

'It makes me want to cry,' sniffed Alison. 'Weddings always do.'

'I know,' Chrissie agreed. 'Me, too. It's the music, I think, and the idea of lifelong commitment to each other.'

'Not something you and I are particularly familiar with.' There was a trace of bitterness in Alison's voice, reminding Chrissie of how Alison had also been more than unlucky in love. 'Never mind, though, there's still time,' she continued on a brighter note. 'Speaking of which, what do you think of the best man?'

'The best man?' asked Chrissie coolly. 'What about him?'

'Oh, come on, don't tell me you haven't noticed him. He's drop-dead gorgeous. I know you're off men at the moment, Chrissie,' Alison went on, 'but even you must have noticed this one. Any idea who he is?'

'Yes,' Chrissie said as they watched the wedding group of Caitlin and Michael, the bridesmaids and the best man line up on the steps of the church as the snowflakes flurried about them. 'He's Sean O'Reagan—Michael's brother.'

'Wow,' breathed Alison. 'That figures. I always thought Michael was dishy but this one—well...' She trailed off, the unfinished sentence expressing her sentiments precisely. 'Have you met him yet?' she added after a moment.

'Oh, yes,' Chrissie replied. 'He's staying at the hotel— a group of us met for drinks last night. I think that must have been before you arrived.'

'What did you think of him?'

'A bit full of himself, actually.' Chrissie wrinkled her nose, recalling how, when she had been introduced to Sean O'Reagan, he had held onto her hand longer than necessary and had looked deeply into her eyes.

'Oh, Chrissie, you're impossible,' said Alison with a laugh.

What Chrissie didn't add was that she hadn't actually been immune to the attentions of the groom's brother, and in spite of herself her heart had beat a little faster during that introduction. But it was the last thing she wanted to admit to Alison and, if it came to the truth, she was loath to admit it even to herself.

'Do we know if he's married?' Alison turned again, her gaze focusing once more on the group on the steps, which had now been joined by other family members.

'Haven't the faintest.' Chrissie shrugged. 'The only thing I do know is that he's a doctor, like Michael. Works in a hospital in Dublin, apparently.'

'The pair of them look just dreamy in their Irish kilts,' Alison observed, and added with a sigh, 'Well, seeing that you've met him, you can introduce me to him at the reception.'

'Looks like people are starting to move,' Chrissie commented.

'It's too cold to hang around for too long—maybe they'll take the majority of the photographs indoors,' said Alison. 'Although, I have to say, I would imagine those in the snow will be quite spectacular—it isn't every bride who has snow on her wedding day.'

They moved towards the fleet of cars waiting on the road outside the church to transport the wedding guests to the sumptuous hotel where the reception was to be held. As they paused, watching Caitlin and Michael drive away in the bridal car, a voice behind them made them turn.

'Ladies, allow me to escort you to a car.' The best man was suddenly beside them. Alison raised her eyebrows at Chrissie, and the two of them allowed him to lead them to one of the cars. 'The snow has added a certain touch of magic to the proceedings,' he said as he opened the door for them to enter the large limousine, 'but on a practical level, we need to keep things moving.'

'See what I mean?' breathed Alison as they scrambled into the back of the car and Sean closed the door behind them. 'He's delicious.'

'I suppose...' Chrissie shrugged.

The drive through the countryside of County Cork was soon over and it seemed to Chrissie that in no time at all they were being welcomed into the warmth of the baronial hall of Ballinsale Castle, where a log fire blazed in a huge central fireplace, the stone walls were adorned with Irish tartans and shooting trophies, and uniformed staff offered substantial aperitifs to drive out the cold. At the wedding banquet that followed, Chrissie found herself seated between Liam Flynn, a cousin to Caitlin, and her own boss, consultant surgeon Oliver Stark, who himself had claims to Irish ancestry, his mother's maiden name being McCarthy. Between them the two men kept her hugely entertained, Liam with his stories and anecdotes of Irish life and Oliver with his rather wishful thinking of what might have been. Alison was seated close by and Chrissie observed that she, too, was being well looked after by others of the O'Reagan or Nolan families.

Chrissie wasn't quite sure at what point it was that she realised that she was being watched. She only knew that gradually a certain awareness crept up on her with the persistence of a sea mist. It happened somewhere between the serving of the main course of rack of lamb and the dessert, a delicious concoction of peaches steeped in whiskey and served with chocolate and whipped cream. She'd raised her head, half turned her gaze towards the top table, and her eyes had met his.

Sean O'Reagan was watching her openly and unashamedly, as if he had been willing her to look in his direction, and when at last he caught and held her gaze he smiled, lifted his glass and inclined his head, albeit slightly, in her direction. Chrissie was forced into some sort of response, knowing it would appear bad-mannered in these particular circumstances if she were simply to ignore him. Graciously she allowed the faintest of smiles to touch her lips while she, too, slightly inclined her head.

'I saw that,' mouthed Alison from across the table, and later, after the speeches and the cutting of the cake, while they waited for the music and dancing to begin, she leaned over Chrissie's shoulder on her way to the powder room. 'It just isn't fair,' she muttered. 'There's you attracting all the attention and you're not even interested.'

'I'll try and introduce you when you come back,' said Chrissie with a laugh.

'Just make sure you do,' Alison retorted darkly.

But long before Alison's return Sean had made his way across the vast hall to Chrissie's side. She saw him coming, threading his way through the throng of guests, and she would have been lying if she had pretended that her pulse didn't race a little at the sight of this tall, kilted Irishman with his dark hair and deep blue eyes heading purposefully in her direction.

'Hello again,' he said. 'Mind if I join you?'

'No, of course not,' she murmured as he sat down beside her and she found herself wondering what he would have done if she'd said, yes, she did mind. But at the same time, oddly, she realised that she really didn't mind. How could any woman mind being the object of those blue eyes and that devastating smile?

'I think,' he said, after making sure that she had a drink, 'that I can relax now—my duties are pretty well over.'

'You must be relieved,' she said.

'Do you know, I think I am, to be honest.' He took a mouthful of his drink. 'When I agreed to be Michael's best man, I don't think I had any idea of all that it entailed.'

'Was Michael best man at your wedding?' she asked lightly, then found herself holding her breath as she waited for his reply.

'Lord, no!' he said quickly. 'Not that he wasn't best man,' he added when he saw her raised eyebrows. 'What I meant was, I'm not married.'

Alison will be pleased, thought Chrissie. 'But presumably,' she said aloud, 'if and when you do, Michael will be put through his paces.'

'Well, yes,' he agreed, '*if* being the operative word rather than *when*.'

She smiled. 'You don't intend being caught in the marriage trap?'

'Not if I can help it—at least,' he corrected himself, 'not for a very long time. I'm simply not ready to settle down and take on all that entails.'

'Luckily for Caitlin, Michael didn't feel that way,' Chrissie observed as her gaze was drawn to the dance floor where the bride and groom were starting the first dance. Caitlin's mass of red hair was a perfect foil against the O'Reagan dark colouring.

'Oh, Michael and Cait are different,' he said, his voice softening.

'In what way different?' she asked.

'They've loved each other for ever. There's never been anyone else for either of them.'

'Like you said in your speech.'

'Yes,' he agreed, 'like I said in my speech.'

'I thought your speech was very good,' she said after a moment.

'Well, thank you, but I guess that was probably because I know Michael better than anyone—apart from Cait, of course,' he added generously. Rising to his feet, he set down his glass and held out his hand. 'Shall we join them?' he asked.

Wordlessly she took his hand, allowing him to raise her to her feet, then somehow she found herself drawn into his arms and guided onto the floor.

'As best man, shouldn't you be dancing with someone else?'

'Whom did you have in mind?' he said softly.

'Well, I don't know…but traditionally, I thought…'

'Yes,' he agreed, 'traditionally the best man dances with the chief bridesmaid but, seeing that Caitlin had all small bridesmaids, surely the most appropriate thing is for me to be dancing with one of her best friends?'

'Well, yes, I suppose so,' Chrissie replied.

'And seeing as that friend doesn't seem to have an escort or a partner—that's right, isn't it, you don't have anyone with you?'

'No,' she agreed, 'I don't have anyone with me.'

'And…' he glanced down at her left hand where it lay on his arm '…I don't see any evidence of anyone permanent in your life away from here either.'

'That's right.' She managed a cool smile. 'There is no one.'

'I find that very hard to believe,' he said softly.

'Well, it's true.' She gave a slight shrug. 'There's no one in my life at the moment and, if I'm honest, I quite like it that way.'

They were silent for a while as they moved slowly around the floor to the strains of the music, and quite suddenly and somewhat unexpectedly Chrissie realised that she was enjoying herself. He was a good dancer and she felt secure and relaxed in the circle of his arms. 'You told me last night you work on the same unit as Caitlin,' he said at last, breaking the silence between them.

'Yes, we're both on Surgical at Ellie's,' she said, knowing he would be familiar with the affectionate abbreviation from his brother.

'Do you intend specialising?' he asked.

'Yes,' she replied simply, then, seeing his questioning look, she went on. 'For a long time I thought I would like to go into general practice but then I was drawn towards general surgery, so after much encouragement from Oliver Stark I've decided to go for the post of registrar, which is shortly becoming vacant.'

'I see,' he said slowly. 'Well, good for you—there's a decided shortage of women in general surgery in my opinion.' He paused. 'Do you think you stand a good chance?'

'Yes, I hope so. Certainly if the interviewees are just from Ellie's, I think I stand as good a chance as anyone else. If there are other candidates from outside, the competition may be stronger but...well, we'll have to wait and see what happens. So...' She looked up at him. 'What about you?'

'What about me?'

'Well, you're also in general surgery, aren't you?'

'Yes, I'm surgical registrar at St Luke's in Dublin.'

'Well on your way to a consultancy, then?' She raised her eyebrows.

'Hopefully, yes,' he agreed, 'although I can't see it happening at St Luke's—the consultants I work for are not much older than I am, and it'll be years before either of them retires.'

'Maybe one of them will move on,' Chrissie replied, not without a certain degree of sympathy.

'Yes, maybe,' he agreed, although he didn't sound too hopeful. At that moment the music changed to an upbeat tempo and the little spell that had been woven around the two of them as they'd danced together was broken.

Deftly Sean led her back to her seat, where they found that Alison had returned and was eyeing the pair of them speculatively as they walked across the floor towards her. Chrissie, knowing what was expected of her, turned to Sean. 'I don't believe you've met Alison.'

'No,' he said, 'I haven't.' Introductions followed, then Sean excused himself and said he was going to claim his dance with the bride, but that he would see the pair of them again shortly.

'Honestly,' said Alison as Sean disappeared through the throng of people around the dance floor, 'you really are the limit, Chrissie.'

'What do you mean?' said Chrissie. 'I've introduced you—that's what you wanted, wasn't it? What more do you want?'

'Well, I turn my back for five minutes and when I come back, there you are dancing with him. You certainly didn't waste any time, did you?'

'He just came over and asked me to dance,' said Chrissie. 'It was no big deal—he'll probably ask you later. I think it's all part of his duties as best man.'

'So what's he like—did you find out anything?' demanded Alison.

'He's a lovely dancer,' mused Chrissie. 'You don't seem to find that too often these days. Most men have two left feet...'

'I don't mean that,' said Alison impatiently, 'I mean did you find out anything about him?'

'He's a surgical reg at St Luke's in Dublin.'

'Yes?'

'What do you mean, yes?'

'Well, is that it? We sort of knew that already. Didn't you find out anything else?'

'Let me see, now.' Chrissie pretended to consider. 'Oh, yes,' she said at last, 'I remember now. He isn't married.'

'He isn't married!' Alison's voice rose an octave. 'Ah, well, now we're getting somewhere.' There was an obvious note of satisfaction in her voice, but that was as far as she got for at that moment Liam Flynn erupted out of nowhere and whisked her away onto the floor, leaving Chrissie trying to control her laughter.

And as the rhythm changed once again, this time to a wild Irish reel, it seemed in no time at all that Sean was back by her side, having duly danced with the bride then led her back to her husband.

'It's noisy in here,' he said. 'Let's find a corner and have a quiet drink.'

'All right,' she said, then glanced back at the dance floor.

'Where's your friend?' he asked, seeing the gesture.

'Dancing with Liam Flynn.'

'That's all right.' A smile tugged at his mouth. 'You won't see her again for hours, especially now the ceilidh has started. Liam's relentless on the dance floor—among other things.' He chuckled.

They made their way out of the main banqueting hall to the smaller reception area and bar, where Sean found a quiet corner then ordered drinks for them both.

'That's better,' he said settling himself more comfortably. 'I can hear you talk now.'

'What is it you want me to say?' she said lightly.

'I want to know all about you,' he replied, taking a

mouthful of his drink before setting it down on the small table in front of them. 'But before that, I want to say how lovely you look. I've been thinking it all day. That burgundy colour of your dress really suits you.'

'Thank you.' She spoke lightly but was annoyed to feel the colour touch her cheeks at the compliment. She'd never been good at receiving compliments, usually shrugging them off or brushing them aside, until someone—she couldn't remember who—had pointed out to her that it was better to accept gracefully, and all that was usually required was a simple word of thanks. She'd put a lot of thought into her outfit that day, finally settling on the burgundy satin dress that Sean had just admired teamed with her new camel coat with the fur collar to combat the cold weather. Really, it was somewhat gratifying to have someone admire her choice.

'I have to say, though,' he carried on, giving her no more time for reflection, 'that I'm still finding it incredibly difficult to understand why you're on your own.'

'On my own?' She stared at him for a moment, not understanding, then something about the look in his eyes made his meaning crystal clear, and at the same moment warning bells began to sound in her head. This man was a charmer. She'd suspected it that very first moment that their eyes had met—now she was certain of it, and knew she needed to be on her guard.

'It isn't often I have the good fortune to meet a lovely, intelligent young woman like yourself, only to find that she is unattached,' he said thoughtfully. his eyes never leaving her face as he spoke. 'Are you sure there isn't someone lurking in the shadows, just waiting to leap out if I as much as take even the smallest of liberties?'

'I can assure you there's no one,' Chrissie replied, 'but that's not to say I intend allowing you, or anyone for that matter, to take liberties, however small.'

He frowned. 'You said that as if when you did allow someone to take liberties, they took advantage—am I right?'

'You might be.' Chrissie looked away quickly. She had no intention of offering any explanation to this man of why her last relationship had failed so miserably, but it seemed Sean had other ideas.

'Who was he?' he said, his voice more intense now as he leaned closer to her.

'Who was who?' Chrissie tried to keep her tone even, casual, but feared her emotions were rising as they always did at mention of this particular subject, and that Sean knew exactly that that was happening.

'This man who took advantage of you,' he said in the same quiet tone.

'You make it sound as if I were some vulnerable child in need of protection, instead of a responsible woman in charge of her own destiny.'

'Oh, I don't doubt you were and are a responsible woman,' he said swiftly, and she was forced to return her gaze to his, 'but that doesn't mean you weren't and aren't still very vulnerable. In my experience, when people fall in love they are extremely vulnerable, and if for whatever reason that love ends, they are even more so.'

'Who says I was in love?' she said in a sudden desperate attempt at flippancy.

'Oh, I would have said that was a certainty,' he replied softly. 'I can't imagine you to be the sort of woman who'd be involved in a relationship if love wasn't present.'

'How can you know that?' she demanded. 'You don't even know me.'

He shrugged. 'Intuition? It isn't only you ladies who have the monopoly on that, you know.'

'No,' she agreed, 'maybe not, but—'

'So, am I wrong?' he broke in. 'Were you not in love?'

Chrissie stared at him for a long moment, then she drew a deep breath. What the hell did it matter now whether she told him or not? It was over, water under the bridge. 'No,' she said at last, 'you aren't wrong. I did love him once—of course I did.'

'Ah,' he said. 'So who was he?'

'He was a consultant surgeon on the cardiac unit at Ellie's.'

'Would I have known him?'

'Maybe.' She shrugged. 'His name was Alan Peterson.'

'I think I've heard of him. What went wrong?'

'He went back to his wife,' she said simply. It was amazing how those few short words still hurt so much. When Sean remained silent, she threw him a level glance. 'You're thinking I should have known better in the first place than to allow myself to become involved with a married man,' she said sharply, and when he would have protested otherwise, she raised her hand to stop him. 'And maybe I should,' she went on, 'but the truth of the matter is, when we met I had no idea he was married. After a time he admitted he and his wife were legally separated—and by that time I was in love with him and deeply involved. He led me to believe his wife would divorce him.'

'And she didn't?'

'No.' She paused, then continued, 'And, like I said, he went back to her in the end.'

'Leaving you devastated.' It was more a statement than a question.

'Yes.' She bit her lip.

'Chrissie…' Urgently he leaned forward and took her hands. 'Don't let it cloud your judgement of all men,' he said. 'We aren't all the same.'

'I know,' she said then, managing a laugh, added, 'Some are worse.' It lightened the mood and they went on to talk of other things—Sean's family, where he lived in Dublin and the family home in Cork.

'Is this your first visit to Ireland?' he said.

'Yes, it is, and I have to say I like what I've seen so far.'

'When are you going home?'

'Tomorrow, late afternoon.'

'How about I show you around a bit in the morning?' he said eagerly.

'OK.' She gave a little shrug. 'It may be Alison as well,' she added.

He laughed. 'I wouldn't count on that—not if Liam has anything to do with it.'

CHAPTER TWO

'SO YOU'VE really gone and done it now, haven't you, old son?' Sean grinned at his brother as he helped him out of his wedding attire. 'It's downhill all the way from now on— you do realise that, don't you? It doesn't stop with today's ceremony, that's just the beginning. There'll be a mortgage, then children, and once they come along, no more freedom until they leave home. And even then,' he added darkly, 'from what I've heard, that can be doubtful, because some of them are students till they're nearly thirty, and if and when they do leave home, they keep coming back.'

'You really know how to make a bloke feel good on his wedding night, don't you?' Michael pulled a face as he handed over the family tartan he'd worn that day.

'Just stating a few facts, that's all,' Sean replied airily.

'One or two things you're forgetting, though,' observed Michael.

'Oh, and they are?' Sean began folding the kilt.

'Caitlin and I have actually been living together for some time now, and we took out a mortgage together ages ago—'

'Ah, but that's only part of it,' Sean persisted. 'At least now, though, you've pleased the parents.'

'You wait, it'll be your turn next, you mark my words,' his brother retorted.

'No way—not yet, I can assure you.' Sean pulled a face. 'There's no way I'm ready to settle down, and that's a fact.'

'Well, I know you've played the field,' said Michael with a grin, 'but I reckon the only reason you haven't taken the plunge is because you haven't yet met the right woman.'

'Maybe not.' Sean shrugged.

'Because when you do, there really isn't anything you can do about it—you just know, and there's simply no point in looking any further.'

'How would you know about that?' Sean looked up sharply. 'There's never been anyone else for you but Cait—unless…'

'Unless what?' demanded Michael.

'Unless you've been holding out on me all these years. Have you?' he demanded when Michael didn't immediately reply.

'No, of course not,' Michael retorted. 'I consider myself more than fortunate that I always knew Caitlin was the girl for me, and I've never felt the need to look any further.'

Sean stared at Michael then slowly said, 'Actually, and I can hardly believe I'm saying this, I envy you. It must be quite awesome to be so certain about something as fundamental as that.'

'Your time will come. And by the looks of it you're still having a great time playing the field.'

'Well, that's true,' Sean admitted.

'You certainly seemed to be getting on rather well with our Dr Chrissie Paige today.'

'She is rather lovely, isn't she?' Sean agreed. 'I could hardly believe my luck, especially when she said she isn't in a relationship at the moment.'

'She was, you know,' said Michael thoughtfully as he pulled on the black jacket he was wearing to the hotel where he and Caitlin were spending their wedding night. 'Not so long ago.'

Sean nodded. 'So she said. Some consultant at Ellie's, wasn't it?'

'She told you that?' Michael looked surprised.

'Yes,' Sean replied levelly. 'She also said he went back to his wife.'

'That's right,' Michael agreed. 'I'm surprised she told you that. Caitlin said she was absolutely devastated at the time.'

'Maybe she's got over it now,' Sean suggested.

'Yes, maybe,' Michael replied doubtfully.

'Did you know that she's applying for the surgical reg position at Ellie's?' asked Sean as the two men left the room and made their way along the corridor to the room Caitlin and her bridesmaids were using.

'No.' Michael stopped briefly and stared at him. 'I didn't know that. I wouldn't have thought she was quite ready for that yet.'

'Well, that's what she said,' Sean replied. 'She seems very keen to get it as well.'

'Did you tell her you've applied?' Michael's eyes narrowed.

'No, I didn't,' Sean admitted. 'Somehow I didn't quite have the heart. She seems wary of any outside applicants, and I couldn't quite bring myself to tell her that I would be in competition with her. The thing is, there'll probably be several other candidates and maybe neither of us will be successful—time enough to tell her then.'

'Yes, I suppose so,' Michael agreed, but nevertheless he sounded doubtful.

'I've arranged to see her tomorrow before she goes home,' said Sean as they reached the door to Caitlin's room.

'Oh, yes?' Michael raised one eyebrow. 'Still playing that field?'

Sean laughed. 'If that's what you want to call it.' As Michael opened the door he said, 'Do you blame me?'

'Not at all.' Michael shrugged. 'She's a lovely girl—but, hey, Sean, go easy. Don't go hurting her, will you? I would say she's had more than enough in that respect.'

'Now, would I do such a thing?' There was a look of injured innocence on Sean's face as they stepped into the room and Caitlin turned to greet them. She was wearing a long skirt of emerald green and a tiny fitted jacket in the same colour fastened with a row of pearl buttons, which suited her vibrant colouring to perfection.

'I wouldn't put it past you,' Michael murmured as he turned to greet his bride.

Chrissie stared up at the ceiling and in her mind went over and over the events of the day. She couldn't quite believe that she had told anyone, especially a virtual stranger, so much about herself but somehow Sean O'Reagan had been so easy to talk to that she had found herself pouring out details of her relationship with Alan and of the subsequent break-up, which she had never before discussed with anyone. In the end she had spent the rest of the evening with him. They had danced again, several times, a couple of dances which were typically Irish folk dances—fast, and to the frenzied sound of fiddles—dances which had left her flushed and breathless but happy—and others, slower dances when he had confidently led her onto the floor and wordlessly she had followed, slipping easily into his arms and once again enjoying his expertise as a dancing partner. But as the night had worn on and the lights had dimmed, the music and the dancing had changed yet again and Chrissie had found Sean holding her that little bit closer as they'd merely swayed to the music, barely moving at all.

There was no denying the attraction and indeed the chemistry between them. Once she had guiltily thought of Alison, but then, on searching for her friend and seeing her entwined in Liam's embrace, she'd speedily dispelled those feelings of guilt. The warning bells had sounded again in her head, especially when Sean had rested his cheek against hers—this was the last thing she wanted, wasn't it? But she'd disregarded those warnings also. After all, what possible harm could come of it? It wasn't often that a gorgeous handsome man paid her this much attention, so she may as well enjoy it while she could, and it was only for this one weekend—she probably wouldn't set eyes on him again afterwards.

Later everyone had poured out of the hotel foyer as Michael and Caitlin had departed for an unknown hotel for their wedding night. 'Thought you would have stayed here, Mikey,' called someone in the crowd.

'With you lot around?' Michael was swift to respond. 'You have to be joking!'

'At least it's stopped snowing,' Sean murmured in Chrissie's ear, one arm around her to help keep her warm.

'It's still cold,' she said, trying to keep her teeth from chattering.

'There's a hard frost,' he agreed, as the car carrying Michael and Caitlin slid away from the hotel and down the drive amidst a clattering of tin cans and resounding cheers from the onlookers, and a burst of fireworks set off by the hotel staff.

The party went on for another hour or so then some guests began drifting away to their rooms.

'I think I'll turn in as well,' Chrissie said at last. 'It's been a long day.' There was no sign of Alison or Liam, although both of them had been present earlier to wave farewell to the bride and groom.

'I'll see you to your room.' Sean stood up.

She hesitated. 'There's no need.' Her protest was barely more than a murmur.

'There's every need,' he insisted. He took her hand and escorted her up the wide staircase to the corridors leading off the main landing. 'Which way?' he asked, and when she pointed the direction, he took her right to her bedroom door.

'Aren't you going to ask me in for a nightcap?' he asked, an innocent expression in his eyes that barely masked the humour lurking beneath.

'I don't think that would be a very good idea,' she replied mildly.

'OK.' He shrugged. 'How about a goodnight kiss instead?'

Somehow she couldn't refuse him and somewhat surprisingly she found that she didn't want to refuse. He leaned forward, cupped her face in his hands, bent his head and very gently touched her lips with his own.

To Chrissie's further surprise, it felt good, and far from dissuading him, as she'd thought she would, she found her own lips parting beneath his, and as he increased the pressure of his mouth she did likewise.

'Wow!' he murmured when at last he drew back. 'Are you sure about that nightcap?'

'Absolutely,' she replied, but her voice had sounded shaky even to herself.

And now, after he'd gone and as she lay alone in the vast double bed, she wondered if she hadn't made a mistake. After all, would it really have mattered just this once to have had a no-strings-attached fling? She was certain that was all that Sean would have wanted, and it would have been so easy. She would have invited him in and they would have spent the night together—they were quite obviously attracted to each other, so where would have been the harm? No one else need ever have known, except possibly Alison, who would question her relentlessly, but it wasn't yet clear how Alison herself was spending the night or with whom, so she'd scarcely be in a position to judge anyone.

So why had she sent him away? It wasn't as if she was some inexperienced teenager on a first date. She was a mature, professional woman, for heaven's sake, and didn't mature, professional women know how to conduct such things these days?

The truth was, and she knew it only too well, she simply wasn't into casual relationships and certainly not into one-night stands, which was what this would have been.

Her relationship with Alan had left her bruised, traumatised even, and very vulnerable. She knew that, but she also recognised that this had been the first time since the break-up with Alan that she'd felt anything like even the stirrings of interest in another man. She doubted somehow she was ready for another full-scale relationship yet, so maybe she should have simply gone for the brief and probably very passionate fling that Sean had been offering. So what had stopped her?

She gazed up into the darkness, not even having to pursue the question in any depth, knowing the answer instinctively, knowing that what had held her back was the fear of being hurt again. She simply wasn't into casual affairs. When she loved she did so with every part of her, not just physically with her body but mentally with her mind and emotionally with her very soul. That was what she had done with Alan, given herself utterly and completely long before she'd known he had a wife, albeit one from whom he had been separated. She knew now that she should have pulled out on the day she had learnt of Hillary's existence, but Alan had appeared devastated at the very idea and had set about convincing her that he would be able to obtain a divorce and that in time they would be able to marry. It hadn't happened, though, and somehow Chrissie had recognised that she'd always known it wouldn't. Alan's wife had refused to give him a divorce, and in spite of the situation Chrissie had found herself with a certain amount of sympathy for this woman whom she hadn't even met. If she was really honest, she too had always hoped that when she married it would be a lifelong commitment. She and Alan had begun to quarrel—at first little more than day-to-day bickering and then more serious disagreements, until at last during one such heated argument she had told him she thought he should go back to his wife. He'd disagreed with her at the time, saying the very idea was preposterous, but looking back Chrissie realised that had been the beginning of the end for them. Eventually he'd done what she'd suggested and had gone back to Hillary.

That had been a year ago, a year in which she had desperately tried to put her life back together, and now today, meeting the O'Reagan and the Nolan families and attending the ceremony that would unite them, it had somehow thrown it all sharply back into focus. There had been many times in the past year when she had ached for Alan and the love which she'd thought they had shared, but more recently she had heard through the hospital grapevine that he and Hillary had moved to France where they were trying to rebuild their lives, and she had finally recognised that what they had once shared was truly over.

Her last thought before sleep claimed her was that maybe it wouldn't have mattered if she had agreed to a brief passionate fling with Sean, but that now she would never know because it was too late. Instead, she would have to settle for the sightseeing he had promised her for the following day. And perhaps that wasn't such a bad thing after all. At least he wouldn't be lying to her, pretending that he loved her, only to cheerfully wave goodbye the next day when they parted for ever.

There was a hard frost overnight, freezing the light covering of snow, and the following morning that frost glittered on the bare branches of the trees and across the crisp, neatly manicured hotel lawns in the early pale sunshine. When Chrissie appeared for breakfast it was to find that very few of the wedding guests who had stayed the night had yet surfaced. She found an empty table by a window that looked out over the gardens and ordered fruit juice, scrambled eggs, toast and coffee. There was no sign of Alison, and for the first time she felt a twinge of unease for her friend, who was known to be headstrong, especially where men were concerned. Now, in the cold light of day, Chrissie was pleased she hadn't been carried away and spent the night with Sean. If she had, by now she would probably be dreading seeing him, whereas, as it was, when she caught sight of him across the dining room she found herself returning his smile quite openly. The fact that her heart lurched slightly was neither here nor there—at least she could hold her head high.

Sean saw her as soon as he entered the dining room and for a split second he felt as if his knees might be about to give way. Then she looked up, caught his eye and smiled, and he breathed a huge sigh of relief. He'd thought she might freeze him out after the night before, but she actually seemed quite pleased to see him. He'd been disappointed that she hadn't wanted to take things further—of course he had, any red-blooded male would feel the same, especially over such a lovely woman as Chrissie Paige— but in spite of that there had been something touchingly refreshing over the way she had gently prevented him from going into her room for that final nightcap, which both of them knew would have led to more. He wasn't used to that, not these days. Women seemed so much more liberated now—so much more like men, if he was really honest—and although he accepted that, there had been something about the restraint that Chrissie had shown that had intrigued him, to a point where he was desperate to get to know her better.

All night he had lain there alone in his hotel bed, with sleep an elusive bedfellow, as he had thought about Chrissie and how there had been something about her that had instantly touched him. He thought about his brother Michael and the love he felt for Caitlin, about how Michael had gently chided him, telling him that he would know when he met the right woman because then he would want to settle down. He even found himself thinking about the man that Chrissie had said she'd been in love with, only for him to return to his wife. Michael had lightly accused him of playing the field and to a point he knew that to be right, but he also knew that it was indeed true that he hadn't actually met the woman with whom he would want to share the rest of his life. Unless...

'Hello,' she said as he approached her table. The few guests he'd seen that morning had appeared hungover, but Chrissie looked clear-eyed and lovely, bathed in the pale winter sunshine that filtered into the dining room and highlighted the golden blonde in her hair, which that morning she wore tied back with a black ribbon. She wore a pair of fine wool trousers in a tiny checked pattern and a high-necked cream sweater.

'Hi, there,' he said. He tried to sound casual, but was afraid he sounded more like a nervous schoolboy. What was it about this woman that made him feel that way? He couldn't remember having felt so gauche since he'd been in his teens and unsure of himself—these days he prided himself on his self-assurance and sophistication. 'May I join you?'

'Of course,' she replied. 'Did you sleep well?'

'Like a log,' he lied, as he took his place opposite her then gave his breakfast order to a hovering waiter. 'How about you?'

'Oh, yes,' she replied, and something in the quick way she said it made him wonder if she, too, was bending the truth. 'I was very tired,' she added, as if to substantiate her reply.

'Yes,' he agreed, 'it was quite a day, wasn't it?'

They made polite small talk throughout breakfast then, as they lingered over a second pot of coffee, Sean decided to take the plunge.

'I seem to remember some time yesterday—' he began, and as he spoke he saw her lift her head and stiffen slightly as an animal would that sensed oncoming danger '—that you agreed to spend some time with me today.' He expected her to refuse, or at least to deny all knowledge of such an arrangement, so when she smiled and nodded he could hardly believe it.

'Yes,' she said, 'I did. You promised to show me something of the area.'

'I did indeed.' Inwardly he breathed a sigh of relief. 'But because it's so icy, I'm thinking it might be as well if we stay fairly close to the hotel.'

'So what did you have in mind?' she said.

'There's a rather cosy little pub that I know within walking distance—what do you say that we head for that, then later we could see if the ice thaws a bit?'

'That sounds great.' She stood up. 'I'll meet you in the foyer in…half an hour?'

'Wrap up warm,' he said. He watched as she walked away from him across the dining room and for one incredible moment he felt as if he was on the brink of something momentous.

She met him as arranged in the hotel foyer, wearing the coat she had worn to the wedding together with a scarf, gloves and a black hat which she pulled down over her ears. Together they left the hotel and began walking down the drive, the ice cracking beneath their feet as they went. It was very slippery in places and to Chrissie it seemed the most natural thing in the world to hold onto Sean's arm. He wore a leather coat over cords and a sweater, and she couldn't help thinking he looked every bit as handsome as he had the previous day in his kilt.

The countryside was very still, eerie almost in its ghostly white shroud but at the same time breathtakingly beautiful as the pale sunlight touched crystals of ice in the hedgerows, causing them to sparkle like diamonds.

'It's beautiful,' she said, pausing for a moment, her breath suspended in the cold air as she looked around her at the parkland in which the hotel was set, at the ancient oaks still lightly shrouded in mist and the black iron railings that bounded the park.

'I wanted to show you so much more,' he said, and he sounded disappointed, 'I wanted to show you the farmhouse where I was brought up, the village where we lived—the school, the church. I wanted to take you down to the coast. I wanted to—'

'Never mind,' she said gently. 'I haven't seen any of this either—it was dark when we got here yesterday—and this pub we're going to sounds enchanting.'

'What time does your ferry leave?'

'Six o'clock this evening,' she replied.

'Hopefully by lunchtime this ice will have thawed and the roads will be clearer, otherwise...' he smiled '...you might have to stay another night.'

The pub, when they finally reached it after tramping through numerous country lanes, was every bit as inviting as Sean had promised it would be, with a crackling peat fire and a genial host by the name of Pat Ryan who, together with his wife Noreen, offered them a warm welcome. Together they sat by the inglenook fireplace warming themselves, thawing their fingers and toes and sipping Irish coffee.

Inevitably their talk turned once again to their work and they compared stories of working conditions and swapped anecdotes. Chrissie admitted how much she hoped she would be successful in the forthcoming interview for the post of surgical registrar.

'It wouldn't be the end of the world if you didn't get it, though, would it?' said Sean as he set his glass down on the table.

'How do you mean?' She frowned.

'Well, you're very young and there will be other opportunities.'

'Well, yes, no doubt,' she agreed. 'But I would still be very disappointed if I didn't get this particular post. Especially as Oliver Stark has encouraged me so much that he's almost got me believing the job is mine.'

'Is it all down to him?' asked Sean.

'Not entirely, no,' she admitted. 'The other consultant surgeon on the same firm is a man called Maxwell Hunter, and then, of course, there will be the others who sit on any interview panel—the clinical manager and the administrator, et cetera.'

'And this Maxwell Hunter—do you get on all right with him?'

She wrinkled her nose. 'Yes, I think so.'

'So it sounds like it could be in the bag,' he said.

'I hope so.' She nodded. 'But, of course, you never can

tell, because, as I said before, if the post is advertised outside Ellie's there's no telling what the competition might be.'

'No,' he replied. 'Quite.' He paused, then taking a deep breath he said, 'Chrissie, there's something I need to—'

But that was as far as he got, for at that precise moment there came a squeal of brakes from the road outside the pub, followed by a moment of silence then an almighty crash.

Immediately Sean leapt to his feet. 'What the—?'

Chrissie swung round and looked through the window. Outside she could see that a car had collided with a delivery van.

'Looks like we could be needed,' muttered Sean as he turned and headed for the door.

CHAPTER THREE

IT WAS far worse than she had at first thought. Chrissie could see that as soon as she followed Sean out of the pub. At first sight it appeared that the delivery van must have skidded on the icy road and slewed sideways, with the car, which had been travelling in the opposite direction, hitting it sideways on. To make matters even worse, a second car had crashed into the back of the first one.

'We have injured people here,' called Sean, then turned back to the pub landlord who had followed them, together with two members of his staff and the only other customer who had been at the bar. 'Ring the emergency services—all three by the looks of it. And, two of you, watch out for further traffic.'

Chrissie ran with Sean across the road to the three vehicles. There were four people in the first car and a quick assessment revealed they were all injured in varying degrees. The impact of the crash had pushed all four forward so that the driver and his passenger seemed to be wedged under the dashboard while the two rear-seat passengers both looked as if they'd suffered severe whiplash injuries. It was impossible to open the door on the driver's side, as the metal was twisted concertina-fashion, but even as she looked Chrissie noticed a trickle of blood running through a gap in the metal and onto the road.

By this time Sean had managed to open the door on the other side to reveal that the front-seat passenger, a woman of around sixty, had suffered severe leg injuries. For one moment she still appeared dazed from the impact, then she half turned to the driver and began calling out. 'Jack!' she cried. 'Oh, Jack, are you all right?'

'Try and keep calm,' said Sean. 'Tell me your name.'

'My name?' the woman gasped. 'Helen. But…Jack, my husband—'

'Everything is going to be all right, Helen,' said Sean calmly. 'This lady here…' he indicated Chrissie at his side '…and I are both doctors.' He turned back to Chrissie. 'Check the other car.'

'OK.' Slipping and slithering on the icy surface, Chrissie moved to the other vehicle. There were two passengers in this car—a young male driver and his female companion. Neither appeared to be wearing seat belts, and the driver was slumped over the steering-wheel while the girl seemed to have sustained head injuries as her face was covered in blood. Chrissie spoke gently and reassuringly to both of them, as Sean had to the occupants of the first car, but somehow she doubted they even heard her.

'What can we do?' Chrissie turned at the voice at her elbow and found Pat Ryan, the landlord, beside her. 'I've phoned for the emergency services,' he added.

'How long before they get here?' she asked.

'We're pretty remote here,' he said. 'Twenty minutes to half an hour, I would say, given the conditions today. Can't we get them out?' he added.

'Not all of them,' Chrissie replied, 'I would say at least two will have to be cut out, and others may have neck injuries and shouldn't be moved until the ambulance crews get here with equipment.'

'You have medical training?' asked the landlord.

'Yes.' Chrissie nodded towards Sean. 'We're both doctors.'

'Well, thank the Lord for that.' Pat swiftly crossed himself.

'Unfortunately we don't have any equipment or medication with us,' Chrissie went on.

'So what can we do? There must be something.'

'Yes…' Chrissie paused and looked around. 'Bring blankets and towels.'

Pat hurried away to carry out Chrissie's instructions, and after another few words of comfort to the young couple in the second car Chrissie straightened up and saw Sean making his way back to her.

'What's the story here?' he said lowering his head and looking into the car.

'Not good.' Chrissie turned away so that the couple couldn't hear what she was saying. 'Her injury is probably better than it looks, with all that blood, but I can't be sure. But her boyfriend is badly injured—it looks to me as if the steering-wheel has gone into his chest.'

'The landlord has sent for the emergency services, hasn't he?'

'Yes,' Chrissie said, adding reluctantly, 'It could take up to half an hour, though.'

'Damn,' muttered Sean, 'I feared that. It looks like both drivers will have to be cut free, and I have to say I don't like the look of the older man. We have two with whiplash injuries as well and a woman with severe leg lacerations.'

'What about the van driver?'

'Shocked, but not so much as a scratch on him,' said Sean. Chrissie turned her head and saw the driver of the van sitting on the bank at the side of the road with his head in his hands.

At that moment Pat and Noreen arrived with several blankets and a pile of towels. Sean and Chrissie quickly set about making pressure pads out of the towels, with Sean taking some for the occupants of the first car and showing the landlord how to assist him in staunching blood flow, leaving Chrissie with Noreen to help with the younger couple in the second car. The blankets they distributed between all the victims, including the van driver, in an attempt to stave off the bitter cold.

'Should I make tea for everyone?' asked Noreen. 'Or maybe a nip of brandy would be better in the circumstances?'

'No,' said Chrissie quickly. 'They mustn't have anything—they could well need surgery when they get to hospital, and if they have anything to eat or drink now it could lengthen the time before they could have an anaesthetic.'

At that moment the girl in the second car began sobbing and struggling to get out.

'It's all right,' said Chrissie moving swiftly to her side. 'Don't struggle.'

'I want to get out! I want to get out,' the girl cried. 'Brendan's dead. I know he is!'

'No,' said Chrissie as calmly as she could, 'he's not dead. He's still breathing. He's badly injured but we'll soon be getting him to hospital. Now, tell me, what's your name?'

'Marie—Marie Connell,' the girl replied. With a final struggle she managed to twist herself out of the wreckage of the car and stand up, only to have her legs buckle beneath her. Both Chrissie and Noreen caught her, preventing her from falling to the ground. The gash on her head was still streaming blood and Chrissie took one of the towels and held it firmly against the wound while Noreen wrapped a blanket around the girl. At that moment, Brendan began moaning.

'Noreen, you take this pad,' instructed Chrissie. 'That's right, hold it firmly to stop the bleeding. I'll see if I can help this young man.' Making her way round to the other side of the car, Chrissie saw that Brendan's eyes were closed and his face was deathly pale. Carefully she leaned into the car through the small aperture where the door had once been and placed her fingers on the boy's neck. To her relief she found a pulse—it was faint, but at least it was there. 'Brendan,' she said, 'can you hear me?'

The boy grunted in response. 'You've been injured, Brendan,' Chrissie went on in the same even tone. 'Trouble is, we can't get you out yet, we have to wait for the fire brigade because they have the right equipment. But when they've done that we'll soon get you into hospital—' She broke off as she realised that the boy's eyelids had flickered open and he was trying to speak. Leaning forward again and listening intently, she just made out one word—'Marie'.

'Marie is all right,' she said quickly. 'She's had a bit of a bump on her head but she's OK—you mustn't worry about her. We'll look after her.' That seemed to satisfy Brendan—either that or the fight went out of him again—and he closed his eyes. Closer examination showed

Chrissie that the steering-wheel had indeed become embedded in the boy's chest, as she had at first feared, and she knew it was going to be a race against the clock to save his life.

She had just straightened up in order to return to Noreen and Marie when a sudden shout made her turn round. The driver of the van, who was still sitting on the bank, was pointing to the patch of road that was just visible between the vehicles.

'Look!' he cried. 'One of the petrol tanks has gone!'

Chrissie looked, and to her horror saw that what he was saying was true. Petrol was spilling out onto the road. Immediately Sean left the first car and the passengers he had been helping and came back to Chrissie.

'We need to get as many out as we can and well away from the cars,' he said. 'We'll have to move the couple in the back of that car—neck injuries or not, the woman in the front can move. What about here?' He glanced into the car then must have seen that the young woman was no longer there.

'The girl is OK,' said Chrissie. 'She's over there. The driver is another matter—I don't think there's any moving him until the emergency services get here. What about the driver of the other car?'

'He didn't make it, I'm afraid,' said Sean. 'At a guess I would say not so much from his injuries—rather, his heart gave out.' He paused. 'Come and help me get these others out, Chrissie.'

Together they went to the first car and with the landlord's help they carefully eased the two women from the rear seat, after issuing firm instructions that they were to move their heads and necks as little as possible. The lady in the front of the car, Helen, proved to be rather more of a problem. She was obviously in great pain from the deep lacerations on her legs and what Chrissie suspected was a broken leg as well, together with her obvious distress over the fate of her husband, Jack.

Eventually they managed to clear the area, carefully escorting the injured passengers into the warmth and safety of the pub, leaving only Brendan imprisoned in his car and the body of the other driver at the wheel of his car. Once the passengers were settled in the pub lounge Chrissie realised that Sean was no longer with them. A glance out of the window confirmed her suspicions: he was seated in the passenger seat of the second car beside Brendan.

With a few quick words of instruction to Noreen and Pat, Chrissie ran back out of the pub to the stricken vehicles.

'What are you doing out here?' Sean looked up at her as she approached. 'You go back inside with the others— I'm staying here with Brendan.'

'In that case, I'm staying with you,' said Chrissie.

'Don't be crazy,' said Sean. 'This lot could go up at any moment.'

'That's why I'm staying with you,' she replied stubbornly.

'No, Chrissie,' he said, 'that's madness and you know it. They need you in there and, let's face it, the medical world can't spare two of us in one fell swoop—one maybe, but not two.'

'But—'

'No buts,' he said. 'I'm pulling rank here. Dr Paige, please, go and tend to those patients. They need you and, besides, there's a very good chance the emergency services will turn up before there's an inferno.' As he spoke he took her hand where it lay on the rim of the open car window and pressed it. Looking right into her eyes, he said, 'Go, Chrissie—you know it makes sense.'

There was no more arguing with him, she could see that, so with her hand pressed to her mouth to stifle the sudden rush of emotion that seemed to wash right over her, Chrissie turned and stumbled back across the road and into the pub.

Once inside she busied herself with helping further with the injured, but while she was doing so she was in constant dread that one or more of the vehicles outside would catch fire and explode, taking Brendan and Sean with it.

Helen, the woman with the leg injuries, was distraught by this time, more over the fate of her husband than her own injuries. In the end, mainly to prevent her trying to get outside again, it fell to Chrissie to break the devastating news to her. 'I'm sorry, Helen,' she said as gently as she could, crouching down in front of the woman where she sat on one of the pub benches and taking both her hands in hers, 'but I'm afraid there's nothing we can do for Jack.'

'He's dead?' whispered Helen, the shock registering in her eyes.

'Yes, I'm afraid he is,' Chrissie replied. 'Dr O'Reagan did what he could but it was too late. He thinks Jack suffered a heart attack—probably following the shock of the crash. Did he have a history of heart trouble, Helen?' she asked gently.

'Yes.' The woman's eyes filled with tears as she nodded. 'He suffered from angina, and two years ago he had a bypass operation… Oh, I want to see him,' she said, turning to look out of the window then wincing with the pain from her injured leg.

'I can't let you go back out there for the moment,' said Chrissie. 'Not until the fire brigade arrives.'

'That's right, love,' called the van driver from the other side of the pub. 'There's petrol all over the road—it could go up at any time.'

'But Brendan…what about Brendan?' wailed Marie, and as she twisted away from Noreen in her anguish, fresh blood oozed from the wound on her head and trickled down her face.

'Ah, come now,' said Noreen. 'Don't be getting yourself into a state. The brigade will be here soon, they'll hose down the road and they'll get your Brendan to the hospital. Now, hold still, there's a good girl, and let me stop this bleeding.'

While Noreen coped with Marie, Chrissie turned her attention back to Helen, trying to staunch the blood from the ugly gash in her leg, which was pumping out over the carpet at an alarming rate. 'Come on, Helen,' she said. 'I want you to lie down here on these cushions—that's right—and I'm going to raise your leg up like this onto the rung of the chair.' Chrissie knew she had to do something and do it quickly. It was quite obvious that Helen's blood pressure was falling rapidly due to the loss of blood. Pulling her scarf from around her neck, she folded it lengthways in half then slipped it beneath Helen's thigh and tied both ends in a firm knot, forming a tourniquet. Anxiously she watched the wound and within a very short time was relieved to see that the gush of blood turned to a trickle then just a faint oozing.

'How is she?' Pat was suddenly at Chrissie's side, peering anxiously down at Helen.

'OK for the moment,' said Chrissie. 'I've managed to stop the bleeding.'

'One of the women who were in the back of the car is in a tremendous amount of pain,' said Pat.

'Try to persuade her to keep as still as possible,' said Chrissie. Lifting her head, she added, 'What's that noise?'

'It's the Garda,' said Pat, looking out of the window, 'and I can see a fire engine and a couple of ambulances coming up the hill.'

'Thank God for that,' murmured Chrissie under her breath.

Events moved rapidly after that as the fire brigade hosed down the road and eliminated the threat from the spilt petrol and several paramedics swarmed into the pub. Then the brigade set up the equipment and began cutting Brendan from the wreck of his car. One of the paramedics recognised Sean, and after Chrissie had been introduced the team was only too pleased to have the services of the two doctors as the injured were transferred to the waiting ambulances. Neck braces were fitted onto the two women with whiplash injuries, and they were able to walk to the vehicles, as was Marie after dressings were applied to her head wound. A little more attention was required in Helen's case, including splints to immobilise her leg, but it was agreed not to remove the tourniquet that Chrissie had applied until they reached the hospital where, no doubt, Helen would be taken straight to Theatre.

Work on Brendan took much longer and the first ambulances had left the scene of the accident long before he was finally cut free. The steering-wheel had entered his chest and apparently punctured a lung, causing his breathing to be noisy and laboured. The paramedics supplied oxygen and painkilling injections that Sean administered before the boy was carried away from the wreckage to an ambulance. While all this was going on, Jack's body was removed in a plain police vehicle.

Sean joined Chrissie, who was standing quietly by the side of the road, watching the van as it drove away. One of the paramedics closed the ambulance doors. 'Are you OK?' he said.

'Yes, fine,' she said with a little sigh. 'I was just thinking how sad that is. One moment that couple were probably thinking of nothing more important than their Sunday lunch and the next—well, life as they knew it was suddenly at an end.'

'I know.' Sean nodded in agreement. 'These things can happen in a split second.'

'His wife said he had a history of angina and that he'd had bypass surgery a while ago.'

'In that case, what happened really doesn't surprise me,' said Sean. 'I would say his heart stopped seconds after impact.'

'You don't think it could have been the other way round?' asked Chrissie thoughtfully.

'You mean his heart attack caused the pile-up?'

'Yes.'

Sean shook his head. 'No,' he said, 'I don't. I can't be sure, of course, but my guess is that investigation will show that the van skidded on the icy road right into the path of Jack's car.'

'And Brendan?'

'Travelling much too fast, especially in these conditions.'

'Do you think he'll be all right?' asked Chrissie.

'Hard to say—but I would think if they get him into Theatre quickly he should stand a chance. How was the other woman by the way?'

'Jack's wife Helen, you mean?'

'Yes.'

'I would say she'd fractured her femur and nicked an artery into the bargain.'

'What did you do?'

'Applied a tourniquet with my scarf—it was the only thing I could do. She was losing a lot of blood and her pressure was dropping.'

'Come on, you two.' A sudden shout made them turn. Pat was beckoning to them from the pub doorway. 'Hot drinks and food on the house.'

They stayed at the pub for over another hour, accepting the welcome hospitality of Pat and Noreen, then Sean saw Chrissie glance at her watch and he knew their time together was almost at an end.

'I shall have to go,' she said, 'otherwise the transport will leave for the ferry without me.'

He sighed. 'Nothing worked out quite as I had planned today,' he said. 'First the weather, then all this…'

'Never mind,' she said quickly. 'None of us knows what's round the next corner—quite literally, in this case,' she added ruefully. She paused, then went on, 'Do you think we did all we could?'

'Oh, yes,' he replied, 'I think so. We couldn't have done any more, certainly not for Jack and, well, no one could have done anything for Brendan until he was cut free. No, considering we didn't have any equipment or anything with us, I think we did all we could. Actually…' He trailed off and Chrissie glanced at him.

'Yes?' she said, raising her eyebrows.

'I thought we worked rather well together, didn't you?'

'Well, yes, I suppose we did,' she agreed. 'The thing is, in those circumstances you don't even have time to think about things like that.'

'Are you saying that in other circumstances it might be different—say, in Theatre, during surgery, that we wouldn't work that well together?'

'No, I wasn't necessarily meaning that,' she said quickly, and he noticed a faint flush of colour in her cheeks.

He smiled. 'One thing that did occur to me was that we should all live for the moment—seize the day, so to speak. Life is too short to indulge in missed opportunities.' Meeting her gaze, he knew she had taken his meaning and was aware that he was referring to the previous night. She was saved from having to answer, however, by Noreen, who came to their table to clear the crockery.

'So, tell me,' Noreen said looking from one to the other of them, 'you aren't from around here, are you?'

'Well, I was, originally,' said Sean, 'but I live in Dublin now.'

'And your wife—where is she from? Isn't that an English accent I detected?' Noreen looked at Chrissie.

'It is indeed an English accent,' said Sean with a chuckle, 'but Chrissie isn't my wife.'

'Really?' Noreen looked amazed. 'I could have sworn…' She tailed off, then said, 'So what are the pair of you doing here?'

It was Chrissie who answered, quite swiftly, so that, Sean suspected, there would be no further confusion.

'We were here for a wedding,' she said.

'A wedding, you say?' Noreen's interest was further aroused.

'Yes, my brother's, as a matter of fact,' said Sean.

'He married my friend Caitlin,' added Chrissie. 'They had the reception up at the hotel.'

'Well, I never. And you say you are both doctors?' Once again Noreen looked from one to the other.

'Yes. I'm at St Luke's in Dublin,' said Sean, 'and Chrissie here is at a hospital in Franchester in the South of England.'

'But the pair of you—not married, you say? But surely you're…?' Noreen spread her hands.

'What would you say, Noreen, if I told you we hadn't set eyes on one another until the day before yesterday?' said Sean.

Noreen looked astounded at his words. 'I would never have believed you,' she said at last. 'Why, I could have sworn…' Shaking her head in disbelief, Noreen went back to the kitchen.

'We must look like an item,' said Sean softly, his gaze meeting Chrissie's.

'I would think it was an easy mistake to have made.' Chrissie stood up, making a show of putting on her coat in what was an obvious attempt to cover her confusion. 'After all, we arrived together and they soon found out we were both doctors so I would guess it seemed quite logical to assume…'

'Nothing to do with the fact that we look good together?' Sean pulled on his own coat, then both of them turned to take their farewell of Pat and Noreen and their staff.

Sean had asked Pat to call a taxi for them and it seemed in no time at all they were back at the hotel, where they found the rest of Chrissie's party loading luggage into the minibus that had been hired to take them to the ferry.

'So this is goodbye,' said Chrissie as she turned to Sean in the final moments before boarding the bus.

'You can never be certain of that,' he said lightly, taking her hands and looking down into her face. 'Take today, for instance, and the unexpectedness of events. And if that leaves you in any doubt, just take a look at those two over there. They hadn't set eyes on each other before this weekend but just look at them now.'

Chrissie turned and looked across the hotel forecourt to where Alison and Liam were locked in a passionate embrace. 'I wondered where she had got to,' she said wryly.

'Now you know,' he replied. 'I doubt they've seen the light of day until now, let alone dealt with a traffic pile-up.'

'Well, just think how much better use we've put our time to.'

'Oh, I don't know…' he began.

'Goodbye, Sean.' Reaching up on tiptoe, she gently kissed his mouth, silencing anything further he might have been about to say.

'I don't like goodbyes,' he said. 'They're too final—the French say it much better.'

'All right, then—*au revoir*,' she said a little breathlessly.

Lowering his head, he whispered the French farewell, then placed his lips over hers and drew her into the circle of his arms.

CHAPTER FOUR

'I THINK I'm in love.' Alison wriggled down in her seat on the minibus with a look of utter bliss on her face.

'I hope this isn't another of your grand passions,' observed Chrissie as the bus rounded a bend in the drive, and the hotel and Sean O'Reagan and Liam Flynn were no longer in sight.

'No.' Alison shook her head. 'This is the real thing, I just know it is.'

'You said that last time,' said Chrissie. 'And the time before, and the time before that.'

'I know, I know.' Alison gave a rueful grin. 'But this is different, I know it. This really is the real thing.'

'So where does it go from here?' Chrissie settled down in her seat, aware as she did so of a rather strange feeling in the pit of her own stomach—a sort of emptiness, an ache that she couldn't quite define. 'I mean, it's not exactly as if you live next door to each other, is it?'

'No,' Alison agreed, somewhat reluctantly, Chrissie thought, as if she didn't want the slightest obstacle to cloud the horizon. 'I know that, but he said he plans to come over to England to see me just as soon as he's able to get away.'

'So what does he do?' Chrissie frowned. For some reason she was finding it rather difficult to concentrate on what Alison was saying. 'Is he a doctor as well?'

'No, he's a farmer.' Alison gave a little sigh as if the very idea of a man of the land directly appealed to her. 'He's a cousin of Caitlin's, as you know, and he's very involved with the running of the family estate.' She paused. 'He's gorgeous, Chrissie,' she went on at last. 'And I *knew* as soon as I set eyes on him.'

'If I remember correctly,' Chrissie replied dryly, 'it was Sean you thought was the gorgeous one.'

'What?' It was Alison's turn to frown. 'Did I? Well, maybe I did, but that was before I really saw Liam. After that, after he'd asked me to dance—well, there was no turning back, believe me.'

'Well, I'm glad it worked out for you.' said Chrissie, turning her head to look out of the window at the Irish countryside, at fields dotted with whitewashed cottages and lanes bordered by hedges of fuchsia and wild woodbine. The ache inside her seemed now to be turning to a feeling of misery as it slowly dawned on her that she might never set eyes on Sean again. Oh, why couldn't she be more like Alison? Why couldn't she take chances and enjoy living for the moment, instead of calculating everything and looking ahead to possible consequences?

'But what about you?' said Alison, breaking into her thoughts and not allowing her any further time for either reflection or recrimination.

'Me?' Chrissie slowly turned her head. 'What about me?'

'Well, you and Sean, of course. How did you get on?' Alison paused, the silence significant in itself, then she said, 'Did I see you come back in a taxi with him?'

'Yes, you did,' Chrissie admitted.

'Where had you been?' Alison demanded. 'Don't tell me you went and spent the night somewhere else with him?' Her eyes widened as if she herself couldn't quite believe that.

'No, I won't tell you that, because it wouldn't be true,' said Chrissie with a little sigh.

'So where had you been?' Alison quite clearly wasn't going to let the matter rest there.

'We went to a little pub for lunch.'

'Oh.' Alison looked disappointed. 'Is that all? I thought you'd been somewhere exciting or wildly glamorous.'

'Like where?'

'Oh, I don't know.' Alison shrugged. 'I thought maybe he'd whisked you away to his home or somewhere. These Irishmen can be quite masterful and romantic when they put their minds to it.'

'Really?' Chrissie raised her eyebrows.

'You mean you didn't find that out?' Alison's expression was quite comical and at any other time Chrissie would have laughed, but at that particular time the last thing she felt like was laughing.

Alison, it seemed, had no inclination to let the matter rest. 'What about last night?' she went on relentlessly.

'What about last night?' Chrissie feared her attempt at casualness wasn't very convincing.

'Well, didn't you...? You know.' Alison began to sound a bit exasperated and, almost rounding on Chrissie, she said, 'You're not telling me nothing happened! You seemed to be getting on so well! I thought—'

'I know what you thought, Alison,' Chrissie replied calmly, 'and I'm sorry to disappoint you, but absolutely nothing happened last night, I can assure you of that.'

'Nothing?' Alison stared at her then rolled her eyes. 'Honestly, Chrissie,' she said, 'you're hopeless. A gorgeous hunk like that and he was obviously interested in you, and you tell me nothing happened!'

'Well, not what you're thinking.'

'Ah, so something did happen—is that what you're saying?' Alison seized on her slight change of tone, and Chrissie knew her friend wouldn't be satisfied until she at least told her something.

'We talked a lot,' she said at last, reflecting on how she'd told Sean all about Alan, marvelling even now at how she could have done so on such short acquaintance.

'What about?'

'Everything really,' she replied. 'Our lives, backgrounds, families, jobs—you know, all the usual. I even found myself telling him about Alan,' she confessed, and then, after a quick glance at her friend, realised that Alison didn't seem to think that was such a big deal, and found herself wondering why she herself had thought so.

'So what else?' Alison went on after a moment.

'Well, we danced together—quite a lot, actually.'

'And?' Alison clearly wasn't going to leave it there.

'He kissed me goodnight…'

'Hah! Now we're getting somewhere.' Alison punched the air in satisfaction. 'So what happened next?'

'Nothing,' Chrissie protested. 'I told you.'

'Right,' said Alison slowly. 'So let's get this straight. You're telling me that Sean O'Reagan—who, from what I've heard, has got something of a reputation as a charmer and a heartbreaker—went to all the trouble of chatting you up for the entire evening, only to give you a kiss, then call it a night?'

'Well, not exactly.' Chrissie began to feel uncomfortable. 'He would have taken things further if he'd been given half the chance, but I wasn't prepared to.'

'Oh, honestly, Chrissie.' Alison stared at her. 'I don't understand you sometimes.'

'Well, I'm sorry, but that's just the way I am,' Chrissie retorted. 'I've never been able to fall into bed with someone I've just met, and that's that.'

'But he still wanted to see you this morning?' asked Alison slowly.

'Yes, he did,' Chrissie admitted. 'In fact, he seemed more keen than ever, and if it hadn't been for what happened at the pub I think we might have made a few plans for the future. As it was…' She shrugged. 'There was no time for anything else.'

'What do you mean? What happened at the pub?' Alison narrowed her eyes.

'There was a road traffic accident outside the pub,' Chrissie explained, 'and obviously, being the only medics on the scene, Sean and I did what we could to help.'

'Was anyone badly injured?'

'Oh, yes.' Chrissie found herself explaining what had happened and telling Alison about Marie and Brendan, about Helen and her husband Jack and the others, and about Pat and Noreen and their kindness.

'Well!' Alison looked quite taken aback when she had finished. 'You don't do anything by halves, do you?'

'It just happened,' Chrissie said. 'It was just one of those things where we happened to be in the right place at the right time…' She trailed off, then threw Alison a sidelong glance. 'What did you mean about Sean being a charmer and a heartbreaker?'

'Thought you might want to know more about that,' said Alison with a grin.

'How did you find out? Who told you?' Suddenly it was very important that she knew more, which, when she thought about it, was pretty crazy, especially about someone she'd probably never set eyes on again in her entire life.

'Liam said,' Alison replied. 'He said Sean had always attracted women like bees to a honeypot and whereas Michael had only ever wanted Caitlin, Sean was the exact opposite and had left a trail of broken hearts right across Ireland. I must admit, when he said that, I was a bit concerned about you.'

'Why?' Chrissie frowned.

'Well, you're different from me, Chrissie. If you fall for someone, you fall really hard. Look how hurt you were after Alan.'

'I know,' said Chrissie softly, 'but you needn't have any fears on my account where Sean O'Reagan is concerned. We spent a pleasant time together but, really, that's all there was to it. And, anyway, you're a fine one to talk.'

'What do you mean?' Alison looked affronted.

'Well, only half an hour ago you were saying you were in love!'

'Yes, I did, didn't I?' Alison laughed. 'But I'm realistic enough to know that could be the end of it. I rather hope it might not be,' she added with a wry look, 'but if it is then I can simply say, well, it was good at the time.'

By the time Chrissie reached home, she was wishing she could be more like Alison, wishing she could have seized the day, so to speak, and enjoyed a brief, passionate interlude with Sean. But she knew that if she had, she would have found herself involved with him, and once again she would have been desperately hurt when it came to nothing, as it surely would have done. As it was, nothing had happened, and now that she was home she could simply dismiss him from her thoughts.

So if that was the case, why was it that he still filled every waking moment? Why was it that an image of his face was right there in her mind and the sound of his voice filled her head? He had filled her senses to such an extent that on the ferry she had thought she'd caught a glimpse of him at a corner table on one of the passenger decks. She'd been on her way back from the buffet bar with a tray laden with drinks and packets of sandwiches for herself and Alison, but suddenly it had become important to see the man who had been sitting with his back to her, reading a newspaper. He had worn a leather jacket, just like Sean, and his dark hair had curled slightly at the collar, just as his did. Had some miracle taken place and he had managed to catch the same ferry to England? She'd had to know so, still carrying her tray, she'd made her way across the deck, lurching slightly with the roll of the waves until she'd reached the man.

It was him! She was convinced by the time she reached his side, then he looked up and she found herself staring down not into a pair of familiar blue eyes but into brown ones.

'I…I'm so s-sorry,' she stammered in confusion. The man looked nothing like Sean and a wave of disappointment hit her like a sledgehammer. 'I thought…I thought you were someone else.'

'Sorry…I'm not,' he said in amusement, 'but you're

welcome to join me.' He indicated the empty chair opposite him.

'Oh, no, really. Thank you.' Chrissie, usually so self-
assured and composed, was covered in confusion.
'I'm…with someone.'

'OK.' He shrugged and went back to his paper while
Chrissie turned and hurried back to Alison as fast as the
laden tray would allow her.

'I wondered where you'd got to,' said Alison a minute
later.

She was on the verge of telling her friend then something stopped her—how could she explain how euphoric
she'd felt when she'd thought it was Sean, how desperate
when she'd had to find out, then how disappointed when
she'd realised her mistake? It would have sounded too
ridiculous for words and would have only encouraged
Alison to speculate even further about her feelings for
Michael's brother.

And now she was home and still he filled her thoughts
to such an extent that she began to question her feelings,
and by the time she got to bed she really was wishing she
had spent the night with him and to hang with the consequences. At least that way she would now know what it
was like to have Sean make love to her instead of this desperate feeling that quite simply wouldn't go away.

He couldn't get Chrissie out of his mind. She was there
all the time, every gesture, every image, every mannerism.
The impact she'd had on him astounded him. He couldn't
remember ever feeling quite this way about a woman before, especially on such short acquaintance, and even more
especially on the level of intensity between them. A few

slow dances, talking together and a couple of all-too-brief kisses, and that was all. He would have spent the night with her, given the chance, he knew that, but she had refused him and somehow that had intrigued him far more than if she had allowed him to make love to her. Maybe if she had, that might have been an end to it, although somehow he doubted it. Somehow he suspected that one night with Chrissie would not have been nearly enough. As it was now, though, he was still desperate to know.

The day that they had spent together, too short as it had been, had also been something of a disaster, with first the weather putting paid to the places he'd wanted to show her and then, after settling for second best, their all-too-brief time at the pub being shattered by the accident. And yet… He was forced to admit there had even been something about that that had intrigued and touched him in some way. How Chrissie had dealt with the whole episode, her calm, unhurried manner, her expertise—and the compassionate way she had dealt with the victims had really moved him. She was a doctor, he knew, and her competence at such a time should not have surprised him, but her actions had somehow gone beyond mere competence. And then there had been that moment when she hadn't wanted to leave him in the car beside Brendan when there had been a danger of it blowing up. Maybe she would have reacted in that way with anyone, but she had gone one stage further when she had said that if he was going to stay, she was staying with him. What had all that been about? Could it be that she really cared about him? Could it be that if they had been able to spend more time together, the chemistry between them—and there had been chemistry, he was certain of that—might have developed into something more?

But now she'd gone, back to her life and her friends and her job in England, and such had been the haste and confusion at the time of their parting that Sean had only realised after she'd gone that he didn't have as much as a phone number for her.

He would see her again when he went to England for his interview—he would make sure of that—but he wasn't certain he could wait that long. Reaching for his mobile phone, he dialled a number. His brother answered on the fourth ring.

'Michael—sorry to bother you, but I was wondering whether you or Caitlin has a phone number for Chrissie.'

'Sean—I'm on my honeymoon!'

'Yes, I know, sorry about that, but this is something of an emergency.'

'Oh? What sort of emergency?' Michael sounded suspicious.

'Simply that I'm unable to contact her,' Sean replied smoothly.

'Yes, I thought it might be something like that,' Michael replied wryly. 'No doubt you'll see her when you have your interview…'

'Yes, no doubt,' Sean agreed, 'but I'm not sure I can wait that long.'

'Now, why doesn't that surprise me?'

'I knew you'd understand,' said Sean with a chuckle.

'I'll get the number from Caitlin.' There was a note of resignation in Michael's voice, as if he was well used to his brother. 'I expect she'll have it.'

'Thanks, Michael—I owe you one.'

Moments later he was in possession of Chrissie's telephone number and even though it was very late he tapped out the digits on his phone. She answered almost immediately, and at the sound of her voice his heart leapt.

'I wanted to make sure you got home safely,' he said.

'Oh,' she said. 'Oh, yes, I'm fine. But…how did you know my number?'

'There are ways,' he replied with a laugh.

'I hope you haven't been bothering Michael and Caitlin on their honeymoon,' she said, and there was a touch of severity in her tone.

'As if I would,' he said lightly, then, changing the subject, he went on, 'I thought you might also like to know that I rang the hospital for news of the injured people.'

'What did they say?' She sounded concerned now.

'Well, at first they were reluctant to tell me anything, then when I was able to convince them that I was indeed one of the doctors who'd helped at the scene—'

'How did you do that?' she interrupted.

'I know a doctor who works at that hospital and he was able to vouch for me,' he explained.

'So what did they say?'

'Helen has multiple fractures but her condition is stable after surgery.'

'And Brendan?'

'More serious, I'm afraid. He had severe injuries to his chest and a collapsed lung. He was still in Theatre when I phoned.'

'And the others?'

'Minor injuries and shock—sounds like they are all OK, though.'

'Except for Jack,' Chrissie observed.

'Yes,' he agreed, 'except for Jack.' He paused. 'Was your friend Alison all right?'

'In what way all right?'

'Well, she seemed to be welded to Liam when I saw the pair of them.'

Chrissie laughed, a low sexy laugh that sent a shiver down his spine. 'She says she's in love.'

'Really?'

'But I don't read too much into that—Alison falls in love quite frequently.'

They chatted on for a while about the wedding, some of the guests and the hotel, then Sean said, 'Well, I suppose I'd better let you go, but if it's all right with you, I'll keep in touch.'

'Yes, of course,' he heard her say, and his heart leapt again. 'I should like that.'

They said good night then, and afterwards Sean lay on his bed, staring up at the ceiling. He was glad he'd phoned. It had been wonderful to hear her voice and she hadn't seemed in any way annoyed that he had obtained her phone number from Caitlin. He'd almost told her about him coming to England for the interview in a little over ten days' time, but once again something had stopped him. It was almost as if once he knew there would be an automatic barrier between them, and that was something he really didn't want. Time enough for that when the time came. And, really, he didn't think he had that much chance of getting the job of registrar at Ellie's, which, no doubt, would go to someone already on the staff. Someone like Chrissie, he thought. She hadn't made any bones about how keen she was to get the job and in one way, for her sake, he hoped she did, but in another, if the job went to him it would mean he could be near her. On the other hand, maybe neither of them would be lucky, in which case he would have to think again.

He knew, as far as he was concerned, it was time for a change, not only because, as he had explained to Chrissie, any chance of a consultancy in his present position was very slim, but also because he felt restless. He wasn't entirely sure of the reason for this restlessness, unless it had something to do with Michael getting married and settling down, whereas for him, well, he'd never come close to even wanting to settle down. He wasn't entirely sure why, although he was beginning to suspect that what his brother had said was true: that in the past he'd never met a woman with whom he'd wanted to spend the rest of his life.

Unless... He stirred slightly and linked his hands behind his head. Could he have found the right woman now? Could it be that some miracle had occurred that weekend and that Chrissie was that woman? Almost immediately he tried to dismiss the thought. He was being ridiculous. After all, what did he know about her? They'd spent very little time together and she hadn't really given any indication that she even fancied him. Oh, they'd kissed, but, then, there had been a lot of that going on, as there usually was at weddings. Certainly she hadn't been too keen on taking things any further. He frowned into the darkness. He wasn't used to having his advances rejected but Chrissie had made it quite plain that she didn't intend on spending the night with him. Was that simply because she wasn't over the guy who had dumped her and gone back to his wife, or was it because she really didn't find him attractive? If the latter were the case, she probably wouldn't ever find him so.

And yet... There had been moments when he could have sworn she was interested in him—when they had been dancing, for instance, and when she had poured out the details of her broken affair, it had been as if she'd really known she could trust him. Later, when he had kissed her, her response had certainly given him cause to hope. But all that had been before she had politely but firmly rejected him.

So was he simply wasting his time? He really wasn't sure but no doubt he would find out once and for all during his forthcoming trip to England.

In Franchester Chrissie was finding it difficult to sleep in spite of the fact that she was feeling shattered after the weekend and the journey from Ireland. She had imagined she would sleep as soon as her head had touched the pillow but Sean's phone call had rendered her wide awake. She couldn't quite believe he had phoned and her heart had skipped a beat when she'd heard his voice. She'd tried to sound casual, matter-of-fact, and she wondered what he would have thought if he'd known about the incident on the ferry when she'd been convinced she had seen him—that he had followed her—and had then been bitterly disappointed to find out it hadn't been him.

She was pleased he'd taken the trouble to let her know the progress of the accident survivors, and really, when she thought about it sensibly, that had been the true purpose of the call. She really mustn't read any more into it than that. He had, of course, said he would keep in touch but, no doubt, that had simply been a figure of speech and most probably she would never hear from him again.

With a little sigh she reached over and switched off her bedside light, but sleep still eluded her and the only images that filled her head were those of a dark-haired Irishman with blue eyes. When finally she slept, it was those same images that haunted her dreams.

CHAPTER FIVE

'RIGHT, Dr Paige.' Maxwell Hunter stood at the side of the operating table, his gloved hands poised over the anaesthetised patient. 'This is a routine cholecystectomy on Anne Owen, who is forty-eight years old. The patient's medical history and the X-ray plates have indicated that a Kocher's incision is more appropriate on this occasion than keyhole surgery. So if you would like to proceed, please.' He stood back, allowing Chrissie, who was assisting him that morning, to step forward to the table.

Taking a deep breath, she picked up a scalpel and made the incision below and parallel to the lower rib on the patient's right-hand side, moving her hand to allow the diathermy nurse, who that morning happened to be Alison, to control the bleeding. Under Dr Hunter's eye she deepened the initial incision through layers of fat, abdominal muscle and peritoneum. She then proceeded to explore the abdominal cavity.

'Any abnormalities?' asked Dr Hunter, peering over the top of the half glasses he wore above his mask.

'No, nothing,' Chrissie replied. Carefully she retracted the patient's liver to gain access to the gall bladder, then examined the bile duct for the presence of stones. 'All clear there as well,' she added, and went on, 'Here is the cystic duct and the artery, so we can proceed with the cholangiogram.'

The scrub nurse passed a catheter to Chrissie, who inserted it into the cystic duct, securing it with a ligature before flushing saline through the duct. The X-ray contrast medium was introduced through a second syringe, then the radiographer, liasing with the anaesthetist, took over and X-rays were taken.

'There are no stones in the bile duct,' Chrissie reported, after studying the plates, 'so I'll close it.'

When she had successfully closed the bile duct, Dr Hunter inspected the site. 'That looks satisfactory, Dr Paige,' he said, 'so if you would like to proceed and remove the gall bladder, please.'

'The gall bladder is packed with stones,' said Chrissie after she had carried out the procedure and further bleeding had been controlled with diathermy. 'This woman must have been in considerable pain and discomfort.' After the gall bladder had been removed and sent off for histology and Chrissie and Dr Hunter had checked that the cholangiogram was normal and that bile was flowing freely into the duodenum, a drain was inserted to prevent haematoma formation or bile collection. Then the wound was closed and sutured and the operation was over.

'Thank you, Dr Paige.' Dr Hunter nodded, then strode off to the scrub room.

'Well done, Chrissie,' said Alison, her eyes meeting Chrissie's over the tops of their masks. 'I would say that position of registrar is well and truly in the bag.'

'Thanks.' Chrissie smiled. 'But I'm not counting any chickens yet.'

As the patient was wheeled away to the recovery room, Chrissie herself made her way to the scrub room, pulling off her cap and mask as she did so and shaking out her hair.

Moments later, after washing and changing out of her theatre greens and into her day clothes and her white coat, she was joined by Alison and the two of them made their way to the staff canteen for a cup of tea.

'Have you heard anything from Sean?' Alison asked as she leaned back in her chair and kicked off her shoes.

'Now, what makes you think I would have done?' asked Chrissie, taking a sip of her tea.

'Just wondered, that's all.' Alison shrugged.

'Actually, yes. As it happens, he did phone once.'

Alison stared at her. She seemed to have lost some of her usual bounce in the last few days. 'So when was this?' she asked.

'The night we got back,' Chrissie told her. 'He called to make sure we got home safely.'

'To make sure *you* got home safely, you mean,' muttered Alison. 'I doubt he was too concerned about me, or anyone else for that matter.' She sniffed. 'So what else did he say?'

'Well, he'd phoned the hospital to check out the condition of those people who were injured in that road accident I told you about—he thought I'd be interested to know.' She paused. 'What about you?' she said after a while, when it seemed like Alison wasn't going to say anything further on the subject.

'What do you mean, what about me?'

'Have you heard from Liam?'

'No, why should I?' Her tone was defensive. 'I wasn't expecting to hear from him.'

'Yes, you were,' said Chrissie gently. 'You know you were.'

'Was I?' Alison shrugged, then with an offhand little gesture she allowed her gaze to meet Chrissie's. 'All right,' she said at last. 'Yes, you're right, I was hoping to hear from him…'

'It's only been just over a week,' Chrissie began uncertainly.

'No, Chrissie, don't make excuses for him. This is my own fault. I do it every time. I leap right in, give everything of me there is to give—and then I wonder why they are no longer interested. I never learn, do I?' She looked at Chrissie and although her gaze was defiant, her eyes were suspiciously bright.

'Oh, Alison,' said Chrissie softly.

'I've come to the conclusion that men simply aren't worth bothering about. Now, let's change the subject,' she went on briskly. 'What time's your interview?'

'Three o'clock.' Chrissie's eyes flickered instinctively towards the canteen clock as she spoke.

'How many are they interviewing, do you know?' asked Alison.

'Haven't got a clue.' Chrissie shrugged. 'I think I'm the only one from Ellie's, but I heard a rumour that there are some from outside.'

'In which case, I think you stand a very good chance,' said Alison firmly. 'Let's face it, they like home-grown talent and Oliver Stark is all for you, isn't he? I mean, you've always been his protégée.'

'Yes, that's true,' Chrissie agreed, but her voice must have registered some doubt.

'You don't sound too sure.' Alison frowned.

'It's Maxwell Hunter that bothers me,' Chrissie admitted.

'Well, I don't know why.' Alison gave a little snort of derision. 'You did an excellent job back there in Theatre this morning. I can't see how even he could have found fault with your work.'

'Maybe not.' Chrissie shook her head. 'But he hovers, Alison. All the time he hovers over me, as if he's convinced that any moment I'm going to make a mistake. It doesn't give me any confidence.'

'I think it's just his way,' Alison mused, 'and I suppose when you really think about it, he has to cover his own back. I mean, if anything did go wrong, he would be responsible.'

'Yes, I know that.' Chrissie sighed. 'But it's the same for Oliver and he isn't like that.'

'Yes, well, Oliver's a sweetie and that's that, but Maxwell is a different kettle of fish altogether. Anyway, I thought you did a really good job today—you came across as very calm and efficient, so let's hope he remembers all that during your interview.'

'Yes, let's,' Chrissie agreed. 'Speaking of which, I suppose I'd better get my act together. I want to go and see Mrs Owen before I get ready to face the board. She should be out of Recovery and back in the ward by now.'

Together Chrissie and Alison made their way towards the wards, then Alison left Chrissie as her shift was at an end. 'Best of luck for the interview,' she said as they paused at the staffroom door.

'Thanks.' Chrissie smiled.

'I think it sounds really good,' said Alison.

'What does?'

'Chrissie Paige—Surgical Registrar.'

'Yes, well, like I said, it doesn't do to start counting your chickens too soon.'

'I'll give you a ring later to see how you got on,' said Alison as she disappeared into the staffroom. 'And in the meantime,' she added, popping her head back round the door, 'I'll be keeping absolutely everything crossed.'

Anne Owen had come round from the anaesthetic and was propped up by a mountain of pillows. 'Hello, Doctor,' she said, greeting Chrissie with a wan smile as she approached the bed.

'Hello, Mrs Owen, how are you feeling?' Chrissie stopped at the foot of the bed and lifted the patient's notes from the bed rail.

'Sore,' Mrs Owen replied ruefully.

'You will be for a time,' said Chrissie, noting as she did so that the observations were all within the accepted limits following the type of surgery that had been carried out. 'But just think,' she went on after a moment, 'those little devils over there won't be causing you any more pain.' As she spoke she pointed to a glass phial on the patient's bedside locker that contained the stones taken from her gall bladder.

'I know.' Anne turned her head then winced at the sudden movement. 'I can hardly believe that they were inside me—no wonder I was getting so much pain.'

'Well, all you need to do for now is to rest and recuperate,' said Chrissie. 'How is the pain?'

'Not too bad,' Mrs Owen replied. 'Sister has given me something.'

'That's good. I'll leave you now to get some sleep.'

'Thank you. Oh, Doctor, were you there in Theatre?' asked Mrs Owen as Chrissie would have moved away.

'Yes.' She nodded. 'Yes, I was.'

'I'm waiting to see Dr Hunter,' Mrs Owen went on. 'I want to thank him, you see.'

With a little smile Chrissie moved away.

'So how did it go? I've been dying to hear all about it.' It was much later that same day, and Chrissie had returned to her flat to find her phone ringing.

'Oh, Alison, do you know, I'm really not sure.' Settling the phone beneath her jaw, she sat down in one corner of her sofa and tucked her legs beneath her.

'Don't you think it went well?'

'Like I say, it was really difficult to tell. I answered all the questions they fired at me but by the end of the interview I was no wiser than when I went in.'

'So who was there?' asked Alison.

'All the usual—Oliver Stark and Maxwell Hunter, of course, and Mustapha Ibrahim—I was a bit surprised to see him, I must admit, although I suppose as he is the other registrar he should have a say in who his new counterpart will be.'

'So who else—the administrator I suppose?'

'Yes, and the two nursing managers.'

'So didn't they give any indication at all?'

'Not really. Oliver smiled encouragingly, as I knew he would, and Maxwell Hunter was as po-faced as ever... Oh, and they actually admitted they had others to interview and that they'd let me know as soon as possible, although I can't see anything happening until after the weekend now. So really that's all I can tell you. It's in the lap of the gods now. I'm going to try and put it right out of my mind now and enjoy the weekend,' said Chrissie.

'Any plans?'

'Not really—just chill out, I think.'

'Maybe we could meet up for a drink and a pizza at Angelo's?'

'Yes, why not? Oh, there's my doorbell. Can you hold on, Alison? I'll have to go down—my intercom isn't working.' Struggling to her feet, Chrissie set the phone down then lightly ran down the two flights of stairs to the hall. Through the stained-glass panels in the front door she could see the outline of someone standing in the porch. Deep down she knew she should have a safety chain on the door, just as she knew she should have had her intercom repaired as soon as it had gone wrong, but living in Franchester with its easy, almost lazy pace of life had made her less than vigilant, and without even calling out to establish the identity of her visitor she opened the door.

Sean O'Reagan stood there.

At the sight of him Chrissie felt her heart turn over. One hand was resting on the top edge of the doorframe and he looked exactly the same as he had in Ireland, the same easy smile as that blue gaze with its hint of amusement lurking in its depths met hers. For a fraction of a second it was as if they had never parted, as if they would pick up at the exact point at which they *had* parted, as if he would put his arms around her and allow his lips to touch hers.

'Oh!' she gasped. 'Sean! What in the world are you doing here?'

'I came to see you,' he said simply.

'Oh!' she said again. For the life of her, she couldn't think of another thing to say.

'Aren't you going to ask me in?' There was a teasing note in his voice now. 'I've come a long way, you know.'

'What?' Still she stared at him as if she couldn't believe her eyes, then somehow she managed to pull herself together. 'Oh, yes,' she said at last, standing aside so that he could enter the hallway. 'Please, yes, do come in.' Closing the door behind him, she led the way through the hall and up the stairs. 'Don't you have any bags or anything?' she asked faintly, half turning.

'I've left my gear at Michael's,' he said.

'Aren't they still on their honeymoon?' She frowned.

'Yes,' he agreed smoothly, 'but they said I could crash at their place. Their neighbour had the keys, they phoned her and said I could collect them from her.'

'That's very good of them,' Chrissie murmured.

'They knew how much I needed to be here,' he said softly, and Chrissie felt her pulse begin to race even faster, if that was possible. Had he really come all this way just to see her? By this time they had reached the top landing, and she led the way into her living room.

'Nice place you have here,' he said, looking around. 'I see you overlook the river.'

'Yes,' she agreed, 'it is nice—I love it here.'

'How long have you been here?' He walked across the room and gazed out of the window.

'Three years,' she replied.

He turned from the window and just for a moment looked as if he was going to say something, then he stopped and frowned.

'What is it?' she asked.

'Your phone,' he said. 'Did you know it's off the hook?'

'Oh. Alison!' she said. 'I forgot.' Crossing the room, she

picked up the receiver. 'Alison,' she said, 'I'm so sorry. Look, I have to go now but I'll ring you back later, if that's all right.'

'You've got someone there, haven't you?' Alison's voice held an accusing note.

'Yes, yes, I have.' Suddenly Chrissie found it incredibly difficult to tell Alison who it was that was with her.

'I heard someone talking to you,' said Alison. 'I thought I recognised the voice—is it someone I know?'

There was no escaping now. 'Actually, yes,' she said, hoping she sounded casual but knowing all she sounded was breathless. 'Would you believe it's Sean?'

'Sean? Sean who?' Alison's voice seemed to have risen an octave.

'Sean O'Reagan.'

'What?' This time her voice resembled a demented squawk.

'Yes.' Chrissie gave a nervous little laugh, fully aware that Sean was watching and listening with a look of amusement on his face. 'You know, Michael's brother.'

'I know perfectly well Sean O'Reagan is Michael's brother,' Alison retorted. 'What I want to know is what he's doing in your flat!'

'I…well… He's here on a visit. He's staying at Michael and Caitlin's place,' she added hurriedly.

'Is Liam with him?' Alison demanded.

'Er, no, I don't think so. Hold on a moment, I'll ask.' Turning to Sean, she said, 'Is Liam Flynn with you?'

'Liam?' He frowned. 'No, why should he be?'

'He says no,' she said to Alison, ignoring his question. 'I must go,' she added hastily. 'Speak to you later.' Not giving Alison a chance to say anything further, she replaced the receiver then took a deep breath and turned to face Sean.

For a long moment they simply stared at each other, and in the silence all that could be heard was the sound of ducks on the river below the window. In the end it was Chrissie who broke the silence. 'I forgot I was on the phone to Alison,' she said weakly. 'She'd phoned to see how I got on at my interview and then I heard the doorbell. My intercom has broken so I left the phone and had to go down the stairs…' She was starting to waffle and she knew it, but somehow she couldn't help herself. 'I guess it was the surprise of seeing you there that made me forget…' In her bid to find something, anything, to fill the silence, she began stumbling over her words. 'Er, anyway, whatever am I thinking about? I'm sure you would like a drink…a cup of tea perhaps? Or maybe something a little stronger? Let me see, what do I have—?'

'Chrissie,' he said, breaking into her rambling and causing her to stop dead in mid-sentence.

'Yes?' Somehow she brought her gaze to meet his again, and what she saw there in his eyes silenced her more effectively than any words could have done.

'I had to see you again,' he said simply.

'Oh,' she said.

'I've thought about you every moment since we parted.'

They continued to stare at each other for another long moment, then suddenly Sean moved forward, covering the short distance between them, and before Chrissie had so much as a chance to think what was happening his arms went around her and his mouth came down onto hers in a kiss so firm and thorough that it put paid to any further explanations as to why he was there or what she had felt when she had found him on her doorstep.

They stayed like that for a long time, locked in each other's arms, for all the world like long-lost lovers who had come together again after an intolerable separation.

When at last they drew apart Sean reached out his hand and gently traced the contours of her face. 'Wow,' he said softly. 'I never expected a welcome like that.'

'I've missed you, too,' she whispered, 'and I think about you all the time.'

'Well, what do you know?' He laughed. 'And there was me thinking you might not even want to see me.'

'Why would you think that?' Chrissie looked up at him, giving a little shiver of pure pleasure as he cupped her face in his hands, tilting her head back so he could look deeply into her eyes.

'Oh, I don't know.' He shrugged. 'You weren't too encouraging in Ireland, if I remember rightly.'

'We'd only just met,' she protested.

'And now we're old friends,' he murmured, gently dropping little butterfly kisses onto her cheeks, her forehead, the tip of her nose and even her eyelids. 'Don't you agree?'

'Well, yes,' she replied breathlessly. 'Yes, I suppose we are.'

And this time there was no holding back, no hesitation. The chemistry between them was stronger than ever. By their own admission they had missed each other in the time they had been apart, and had thought of little else, and if there had been any final doubt in Chrissie's mind it was swept away when she thought of how he had come all that way just to see her again.

* * *

They spent almost the entire weekend in her flat, sending out for food when the need arose, talking endlessly over glasses of wine and making love over and over again. Sean was an exciting lover, experienced and mindful of a woman's needs, and briefly at first it reminded Chrissie of those early heady days with Alan. But as the weekend progressed she soon came to realise that Sean was nothing like Alan. His focus was utterly and completely on her and on giving her absolute pleasure, while with Alan she doubted she'd ever had his full attention, knowing that all the time she'd been with him a part of him had always been with his wife.

'You're beautiful, Chrissie,' Sean told her as he stretched out his lean, tanned body above hers, then with fingertips and tongue once again transported her to the very edge of reason. And during his own moment of abandonment, to her utter delight, he called her name.

After each session of love-making they would lie together, satiated and fulfilled in a wild tangle of sheets, then he would settle her comfortably in his arms, draw up the duvet snugly around them and they would talk again.

'I went for my interview,' she told him at one such time.

He seemed to hesitate for a long moment then he asked, 'Did it go well?'

'I'm not sure,' she admitted. 'You never can tell with these things. Oliver Stark was as encouraging as he always is, but Maxwell Hunter is like a closed book. I had been working with him all morning assisting him in Theatre, but in that interview room he looked at me as if he'd never seen me before.'

'Will you be very upset if you don't get the job?' he asked.

'I don't know about upset, but I'll certainly be disappointed. I want to get on, Sean, and I see this as the only opportunity of doing so at Ellie's, at least for the foreseeable future. Still, I can't do any more now, so I'll just have to wait until Monday and see what happens.' She paused and looked up into his face. 'How long are you able to stay?' she asked.

'Oh, I'll be able to stay around for a while.'

'That's good.' She snuggled down against him.

'Tell me,' he said after a while, 'why did your friend think Liam might be with me?'

'I think she just hoped he was,' Chrissie replied. With a little chuckle she added, 'She thinks she's in love.'

He didn't answer and once again Chrissie turned her head to look at him. 'Is there a problem with that?' she asked.

'You could say that.' He nodded and Chrissie noticed there was a rueful expression on his face. 'Liam finds it difficult to commit—he's definitely one of the love 'em and leave 'em brigade.'

'Oh, dear.' Chrissie shook her head. 'Poor Alison, she really does pick them. I suppose that's why she hasn't heard from him.'

'You say she thinks she's in love with him?'

'That's what she said,' Chrissie agreed, 'although with Alison one never really knows. The trouble is that she flings herself headlong into these things without thinking.'

'Not like you, then?' He grinned.

'No, not like me,' she agreed. 'I guess you'd say I was more cautious…although, having said that,' she added ruefully, 'just look at me now.'

'Yes, just look at you now,' he said softly. 'A fallen woman.' As he spoke he moved his hand down under the covers.

'Sean?' she said after a moment, trying desperately to ignore the things he was doing with his hand.

'Mmm?' he said.

'You don't belong to the love 'em and leave 'em brigade, do you?' she asked, squirming slightly.

'Of course not,' he said, an expression of exaggerated shock on his face. 'When I love, I mean it.'

'Well, I'm pleased to hear it,' she said, then with a little sigh she gave herself up once again to the delights she knew were about to follow.

CHAPTER SIX

HE STILL couldn't quite believe what had happened. The purpose of his visit to England had been twofold—his interview for the post of surgical registrar at Ellie's and to see Chrissie again. Both Sean had viewed with a certain amount of trepidation, the interview because he didn't think he had a particularly good chance, and seeing Chrissie again because he hadn't been sure what sort of reception he'd receive. As it turned out, neither had been quite what he had imagined. The interview hadn't quite been the open-and-shut affair he'd thought it might be, and seeing Chrissie had turned into something beyond his wildest dreams.

If he was really honest, the interview had gone rather well, with two things seeming to carry weight in his favour—the fact that he was already a fully qualified practising registrar and his brother, Michael, who was a respected registrar in the same hospital, which seemed better than any referees he might have been able to produce to verify his background and character. The interview board had told him that they had other applicants to see, but they would let him know if his application had been successful after the weekend.

He had been even more worried about Chrissie's reaction to his sudden appearance on her doorstep—once again, Michael and Caitlin had proved invaluable in giving him her address—but once she had got over her initial shock at seeing him, she had practically fallen into his arms. For his part he had been totally overwhelmed at seeing her again and shocked at the strength of his feelings. He had ended up spending the entire weekend at her flat, only returning briefly to his brother's to retrieve his belongings.

Sex between them had been wonderful, he had no hesitation in admitting that much, but there had been more than sex—there had been some elusive quality that he found almost impossible to define but which left him wondering about his brother's comment about instinctively knowing when one had met the right woman. When he was with Chrissie, despite their short relationship, everything felt right with the world, and by the end of the weekend he was daring to hope that she might feel the same way.

He still hadn't told her that he'd had an interview for the job for which she had applied. He knew he should have told her, but because he hadn't done so at the outset it had become increasingly difficult to do so, and over the weekend well nigh impossible. Already he had made up his mind that if he didn't get the job, irrespective of whether or not Chrissie was successful, he was going to leave Ireland and come to England to find work. If by any chance he did get the job, and he still had doubts about that, he hoped that Chrissie wouldn't be too disappointed and upset with him for not telling her, and that she would be happy working on the same team as him.

* * *

On Monday morning Chrissie rose early and showered and dressed ready for work while Sean made coffee and toast for them both. 'What will you do with yourself?' she asked a little later as she kissed him goodbye.

'Don't worry about me,' he said easily. 'I'll find something to do.' And then she was gone, promising she would be home as soon as she possibly could that evening.

An hour later he phoned for a cab, and ten minutes after that he found himself for the second time in three days driving up the wide approach to the Eleanor James Memorial Hospital. The main reception building was long and low with a coral-coloured tiled roof, while the main body of the hospital, the wards, theatres and administration building, were tucked away in a large area behind Reception, hidden from view by rows of conifers. At the front of the building huge macrocarpa trees spread their branches protectively over the mossy lawns and clustering at their roots the first drifts of snowdrops could be seen, bringing an early promise of spring. Several people were around the hospital entrance and Sean sank back into the shadows of the cab. He didn't want anyone he knew to see him before he'd learned the outcome of the interview and had had the chance to explain the situation to Chrissie himself.

Moments later he stepped from the cab, turned up the collar of his leather coat and without so much as a sideways glance hurried into the building.

'No need to ask where you've been this weekend, or what you've been doing, come to that,' said Alison, looking up from the nurses' station as Chrissie approached.

'I don't know what you mean,' said Chrissie. She spoke casually but she felt her cheeks grow warm.

'Huh!' Alison sniffed. 'What I'd like to know is what happened to our pizza at Angelo's.'

'Oh, Alison!' Chrissie's hand flew to her mouth. 'I'm so sorry—I completely forgot.'

'No prizes for guessing why,' Alison retorted. 'And what happened to being cautious and not rushing into anything?'

'Oh, I know.' Chrissie had the grace to look sheepish. 'But, well, it just seemed right somehow…and we had sort of got to know one another, and—'

'Shut up, Chrissie.' Alison was laughing now. 'You don't have to justify anything to me. And I don't blame you. Like I said before, the man is drop-dead gorgeous, and I would have thought there was something wrong with you if you'd gone on holding him at arm's length. Especially now he's gone to the trouble of coming over here to see you.'

'I know,' Chrissie agreed. 'I couldn't believe it when he turned up right out of the blue. And you're quite right about him being gorgeous—honestly, Alison, I haven't felt this way for a very long time. In fact, I doubt I ever have.'

'Well, good for you,' Alison said. 'It's time you had a bit of happiness after the way that louse Alan Peterson treated you. I envy you—I only wish it was me and that Liam Flynn had come over for the weekend.'

Chrissie was saved from making any comment by the arrival of the ward sister, who wanted her to see a patient who had just been admitted.

The patient, Richard Morton, was a middle-aged man

who had been referred by his GP after suffering a number of bouts of abdominal pain and bleeding from the rectum. A subsequent colonoscopy had revealed a mass in the main bowel.

'Mr Morton is for investigative surgery later today,' Sister explained to Chrissie, then turned back to the patient and said, 'This is Dr Paige. She will be assisting in Theatre.'

'Do you have any questions, Mr Morton?' asked Chrissie, as Sister made her way back to the nurses' station, leaving Chrissie with the patient.

'I have dozens,' the man replied, 'but I doubt you will have the answers to any of them.'

'Try me,' said Chrissie.

'Well, for starters,' said Richard, looking her straight in the eye, 'who will pay my mortgage if I snuff it? Who will take my son for his football training on Saturday mornings and who will give my daughter away when she gets married?'

'Those are all hypothetical questions, Mr Morton— may I call you Richard?' said Chrissie calmly.

'Only if I can call you Chrissie,' he replied, peering at her name badge.

'Of course.' She nodded, then carried straight on. 'And they are hypothetical because you are assuming you won't be here to carry out those duties.'

'And there's a very good chance I won't be. Come on, Chrissie,' he said wearily. 'I'm not stupid and neither was I born yesterday. I know what this is—it's the big C, and that means my time is very nearly up.'

'Richard…' Chrissie drew up a chair and sat down beside him. 'You're racing much too far ahead. We don't know for sure yet whether or not you even have cancer.'

'But you have to admit, with the symptoms I have, it's very likely.'

'It's possible, certainly. We know there is a tumour, but even if it is malignant that's certainly not the end of the story.'

'You're just trying to make me feel better.'

'There are many forms of treatment nowadays,' Chrissie went on firmly, 'and there's a very good chance that you would make a complete recovery.'

'So what would you do? Come on, tell me.' Richard leaned back on his pillows. 'You open me up and find there's a cancer in my bowel—what would you do?'

'The first option is surgery,' Chrissie replied, 'to remove the tumour. That would then be followed up by a course of radiotherapy. If for any reason surgery isn't appropriate—'

'If it's gone too far, you mean?'

'Then we would give chemotherapy, followed by radiotherapy.'

'That wouldn't cure it, though, would it?' Richard remained sceptical.

'Maybe not, but it would sure as hell stop it in its tracks and delay its progress,' Chrissie replied bluntly. 'I would have put you down as a fighter, Richard,' she went on, regarding him shrewdly, 'and I'm certainly a fighter. If there's something I want, I go right out and get it. So, how about we fight this together—always supposing, of course, that we actually do have anything to fight?'

'OK.' He looked her right in the eye. 'You're on. We fight. I guess I owe that much to my wife and kids.'

'You owe it to yourself, Richard,' Chrissie replied firmly.

He narrowed his eyes as she stood up and looked down at him. 'Sister said you would be assisting in Theatre today,' he said. 'So, are you a surgeon? I thought Dr Hunter was my surgeon?'

'I'm on my way to becoming one,' Chrissie replied. 'I hope registrar will be my next position, then at some time in the future, if everything works out according to plan, I'll be a consultant surgeon.'

'Good for you, girl.' There was a definite touch of admiration in Richard's eyes. 'You go for it.'

'I intend to,' Chrissie replied with a smile. 'Now, you get some rest and I'll see you later in Theatre.'

'What did you say to Mr Morton, for heaven's sake?' It was later that morning and Chrissie and Alison were sharing a coffee in the staffroom.

'Why, what's wrong?' Chrissie frowned. She was finding it incredibly difficult to concentrate that morning, partly because of the aftermath of the weekend and partly because she was awaiting word from the interview board about her application.

'There's nothing wrong,' Alison replied. 'Quite the reverse, actually. He seems to be in a much better frame of mind since you spoke to him. Much more positive now.'

'Well, that's good,' Chrissie replied. 'I'm glad I've been good for something this morning.'

'I have to agree,' Alison sniffed. 'I mean, after the weekend you've had it's amazing you're here at all.'

'You don't know what sort of weekend I had,' Chrissie protested. 'You're just surmising.'

'Oh, I can guess.' Alison leaned back in her chair. 'Believe me, I can guess. So come on,' she went on when Chrissie fell silent, 'what's he like?'

Chrissie took a deep breath and briefly closed her eyes. 'Chrissie?'

She opened one eye. 'Wonderful,' she admitted.

'That's more like it!' Alison grinned. 'So, come on, I want all the gory details.'

That, however, was as far as she got, for at that moment Chrissie's pager went off and after she'd answered it on the staffroom phone she turned to Alison.

'What's up?' asked Alison in consternation. 'You've gone pale.'

'They want me up in the boardroom,' Chrissie replied. 'Looks like this is it.'

'It's in the bag.' Alison punched the air. 'Just you wait and see.'

'I wish I had your confidence.' Slipping off her white coat, Chrissie smoothed down the jacket of her navy blue suit.

'I would say this is most definitely your time,' said Alison raising her mug as if in a toast. 'A weekend of passion with a delicious new man, followed by the appointment of a dream job. Go for it, girl!'

'Like I say, I wish I had your confidence.' Chrissie grimaced. 'Anyway, I suppose I'd better not keep them waiting.'

Hardly daring to breathe, let alone think, Chrissie made her way to the hospital boardroom and with a mounting sense of fear and excitement knocked on the door.

They were all there, the same people who had interviewed her, and while the atmosphere in the room fairly crackled with tension, their expressions were inscrutable, giving away nothing.

'Come in, Dr Paige, please, and take a seat.' It was

Maxwell who spoke first, then after a moment of deliberation between themselves Oliver took over.

'Chrissie,' he said, and because he couldn't quite meet
her gaze she had a sudden, terrible feeling of foreboding
about what might be about to come. He cleared his throat.
'It is not my way to leave anyone in any undue suspense
so I'll come straight to the point.' He paused and for the
briefest of moments looked decidedly uncomfortable. 'I'm
very sorry, but I have to tell you that on this occasion your
application for the post of surgical registrar has not been
successful.'

She was vaguely aware of Maxwell's blank expression
and Oliver's sympathetic one, that someone shuffled some
papers and someone else inhaled sharply.

'I don't want you to think that our decision in any way
reflects on your work.' Oliver was speaking again and she
had to force herself to concentrate. 'We are all agreed that
we are completely satisfied with your performance.'

'In that case, may I ask why I have been turned down?'
She thought someone else had spoken, but to her amazement Chrissie realised it had been her. The question
sounded far too calm, too controlled for the sudden turmoil she was feeling inside.

Predictably it was Maxwell who answered. 'Quite simply,' he said, 'because there was another applicant more
qualified than you, and it was felt that the team as a whole
would benefit from this applicant's expertise and experience.'

'Your time will come, Chrissie.' Oliver attempted to
placate her. 'You are still very young, and although I per-
sonally felt you were ready for this post, some of my colleagues were not so sure.'

'I see.' Summoning every shred of her dignity, determined not to show her bitter disappointment, Chrissie rose to her feet, only for a wave of faintness to rush over her. Suddenly she needed air. 'Thank you for telling me,' she said to the panel, then she fled.

Outside in the corridor she stopped for a moment in front of a window, her hands gripping the sill until her knuckles showed white, while she took a series of deep breaths to counteract the faintness. For a moment she couldn't quite believe she'd been turned down, but it had happened and she knew she had to face up to it. She was due in Theatre in a little over an hour's time and she knew she would need every ounce of her self-control if she were to prove her professionalism to Maxwell Hunter and continue with the job in hand in spite of her disappointment.

Moments later she was back in the staffroom where Alison was eagerly awaiting her. 'Well?' her friend demanded, her eyes searching her face.

'I didn't get it,' said Chrissie flatly.

'What?' Alison stared at her.

'I didn't get it,' Chrissie repeated with a shrug.

'But why, for heaven's sake?' Alison was clearly outraged.

'There were those who thought I wasn't ready for the job yet.'

'But Oliver Stark thought you were! I mean, he encouraged you to go for it in the first place, didn't he?' Alison's outrage was being replaced by a look of bewilderment.

'Yes, he did,' Chrissie agreed, 'but it seems that someone else applied, someone more qualified than me.'

'And this someone has got the job?'

'Apparently.'

'So do we know who this someone is?' Alison narrowed her eyes.

'No, haven't got a clue. In fact, I didn't wait to find out.'

'Oh, Chrissie.' Alison stared at her and must have seen the gleam of tears in her eyes. 'I'm so sorry.' Stepping forward, she gave Chrissie a hug. 'All I can say is that lot don't know what they're doing—this new bod might be more qualified that you but there's no way they could be more dedicated.'

'I think you'll find expertise wins over dedication every time,' said Chrissie shakily. 'I just hope it's someone I can work with, seeing that they'll be senior to me for the foreseeable future.'

'Maybe another chance will come along soon,' said Alison hopefully.

'I can't see it.' Chrissie shook her head. 'Not in this department, not unless Mustapha returns to the Middle East.'

'Do you think that's likely?'

'Who knows? I'm not sure what I think any more.'

Alison hesitated. 'I was going to suggest a drink somewhere after work—you know, just to cheer you up—but I doubt you'll want to do that. I would imagine a certain someone else will be able to cheer you up much better than I ever could.'

'Oh, Alison.' Chrissie managed a smile. 'You are kind, and it was a nice thought, but I think I will get home if you don't mind.'

'Of course I don't mind. I'd be the same, believe you me, if someone as gorgeous as Sean O'Reagan was waiting for me at home. How long is he staying by the way?'

'I'm not sure.' Chrissie shrugged. 'Michael and Caitlin get back tomorrow so he will probably be wanting to see them.' As she finished speaking she glanced at her watch. 'I must fly,' she said. 'I'm due in Theatre shortly.'

'Heavens!' Alison glanced at her own watch. 'I must go, too—Sister will kill me!'

By the time Chrissie reached the theatre and changed into her greens and her clogs she was feeling better, if only marginally. After she'd scrubbed up she slipped into the anaesthetic room to find that Richard Morton had just been wheeled in.

'Hello, Richard,' she said, smiling down at him where he lay on the trolley.

'Chrissie.' Drowsy from his pre-med, he lifted one hand in greeting.

'So what are we going to do?' she murmured as the anaesthetist inserted a cannula in the back of Richard's hand.

'We're going to fight…' Richard replied with the ghost of a smile.

'Too right we are.' Chrissie nodded. 'See you back in the ward,' she added, but she doubted he even heard her as the anaesthetic took effect and he slipped away into oblivion.

While she was studying the X-rays in Theatre, she was vaguely aware that behind her Richard was being wheeled in and that Maxwell had arrived, ready to commence surgery.

Already she feared the worst for Richard. All the tests indicated the presence of a large tumour in the lower section of his colon, but she hoped that the talk they'd had earlier in the day had made him realise there were several options regarding his treatment and that he was facing whatever lay ahead in a more positive frame of mind.

One of the staff on Richard's ward had told her that his

wife, son and daughter had all been with him that morning before he'd received his pre-med, and that they were all staying in the hospital until his surgery was over. It had also been decided that if it was possible, the tumour would be removed there and then.

She was feeling calmer now, still deeply disappointed, of course, at not getting the post of surgical registrar, but much calmer as she prepared herself to assist the man she suspected had been the one to block her appointment. The one who had thought she was not yet ready for such an appointment.

She turned to face him but found that he had turned away to talk to the anaesthetist, and instead her eyes met those of a second man who must have come into Theatre with Maxwell. There was nothing unusual in that. Very often a surgeon would invite someone else to either assist, to observe, to advise or simply to learn from the surgical procedures being carried out. What was unusual, however, and what stopped Chrissie in her tracks, was the familiarity of the blue eyes that met hers over the top of his mask. It was one of those moments of seeing someone, even someone so dear and well known, in a situation so out of context that the brain almost failed to register what is happening.

'Sean?' She knew her own eyes widened, the shock at seeing him there quickly replaced by a sudden surge of pleasure as she briefly recalled the last moments she had seen him, earlier that very morning when he had just stepped naked from the shower and despite her protests had held her close, soaking the shirt she'd just put on to wear to work, forcing her to change it. All that had happened after mind-blowing early morning love-making...

All these thoughts whirled through her mind even as she wondered if he was thinking the same, but somehow this time she didn't seem quite able to read the expression in his eyes. This time even the amusement was missing. And then the reality of the moment clicked into place and she frowned.

'Sean…?' she said again.

'Hello, Chrissie,' he said, his voice faintly muffled behind his mask.

'But…why…? What are you doing here?'

'I've been invited to observe,' he replied.

'But why? I don't understand.' Her gaze flickered briefly to Maxwell, who had taken up his position next to Sean on the opposite side of the table from Chrissie.

'Ah, yes, Dr Paige,' said Maxwell, and for the first time Chrissie detected a note in his voice which could almost have been one of embarrassment. 'I would like you to meet Sean O'Reagan. Sean, this is Dr Chrissie Paige, who will be assisting me during this operation.'

'Actually, Maxwell.' It was Sean who spoke first. 'Dr Paige and I have already met.'

Already met? Chrissie had to fight an almost hysterical surge of laughter. That surely had to be the understatement of the year after the wonderful, passionate weekend they had just shared.

'Oh, really? When was that?' Maxwell stood back as the scrub nurse began draping the green covers over Richard, exposing the area of his lower abdomen ready for the incision.

'Er…we met in Ireland at my brother Michael's wedding,' Sean explained, being as brief as it was possible to be.

Chrissie breathed an inward sigh of relief. She didn't know what she would have done if he'd told the whole truth in front of the entire theatre staff, that they had actually spent the best part of the last weekend in bed. At least his answer had been discreet, compromising neither of them, but it still didn't explain why he was there, why Maxwell should have invited him into Theatre. Come to that, why hadn't he mentioned to her that very morning that he was coming to Ellie's later that day?

'Right,' said Maxwell, pulling on his gloves, 'let's get on, shall we? Scalpel, please.'

'I'm sorry,' said Chrissie, looking from one to the other of the two men, 'but I still don't understand why you are here, Sean.'

'Oh, I'm sorry, didn't I say?' Maxwell paused and looked up, the scalpel poised over Richard's abdomen. 'Sean O'Reagan is our new surgical registrar.'

CHAPTER SEVEN

AT FIRST Chrissie thought she'd misheard, that what Maxwell had said couldn't possibly be so, because there was no way that Sean could be the new registrar at Ellie's. If that were so, she would have known. He would have told her.

Wildly she looked from one to the other and when her gaze met Sean's he raised his eyebrows very slightly, the gesture somehow endorsing the surgeon's statement. And as Maxwell's words sank in, with a startling sense of certainty Chrissie knew that she hadn't misheard at all and that what he had said was right. Unbeknown to her, Sean had applied for the post, had presumably been interviewed just as she had, and had been offered the position for which she had been passed over.

And then, even as she stood there watching, as Maxwell made the incision and the operation commenced, it gradually dawned on her what a fool she had been. Sean hadn't come to England to see her at all. He'd come for an interview, an interview for the job that she had told him about, the job she had also told him she so desperately wanted. Damn him, she'd even slept with him under the misapprehension that he'd come to England solely to see her.

She didn't know how she got through the rest of that operation—in the end, the only way she could function properly was to block the events of the past few hours and indeed the past few days from her mind and focus completely on Richard and what was happening on the table in front of her. And that included not making eye contact with Sean again or, come to that, even with Maxwell.

Somehow she managed to carry out the duties required of her, but it was as if she performed like some automaton— a robot that had been programmed to carry out specific tasks.

The tumour was the size of a large grapefruit and was situated deep in the colon. 'It doesn't appear to have spread.' It was Sean who made the observation.

'What would be your course of action?' asked Maxwell.

'I would remove it and after histology follow up with radiotherapy,' Sean replied.

'Dr Paige?'

Chrissie wanted to say she didn't know why he was even bothering to ask her when her opinion obviously meant so little but, of course, she didn't. 'I would do the same,' she replied, her coolness, she hoped, reflecting her professionalism.

After further deliberation among the team Maxwell decided to proceed and remove the tumour, which necessitated the removal of a section of bowel at the same time. 'It almost certainly looks malignant,' he said, 'but we need to have that confirmed by pathology.'

At the end of the procedure Maxwell asked Chrissie to close. By the time she had finished both the consultant surgeon and Sean had left the theatre, Sean no doubt borne away for talks with his new superior. Utterly exhausted, not only by the physical and mental intensity required for the surgical procedure that had just been undertaken but also by the emotional turmoil that had ensued from Sean's appearance, Chrissie tore off her cap and mask and shook out her hair, before changing from her theatre greens into her suit.

Officially she was now off duty, but before leaving the hospital she slipped into the ward to see Richard. When she arrived it was to find that he had just been brought back to the ward from Recovery, but was still sleeping off the effects of the long anaesthetic that had been necessary for his surgery. His wife was beside his bed and she looked up questioningly at Chrissie.

'How did it go?' she asked. She looked exhausted, with dark circles around her eyes.

'It went well,' Chrissie replied. 'There was a tumour—but we knew that,' she added. When Richard's wife nodded, she went on, 'We removed it and it's gone off to pathology to see whether or not it's cancerous. We also had to remove a section of bowel.'

'A colostomy?' said Mrs Morton quickly, and when Chrissie nodded she said, 'Dr Hunter said that might be necessary—so Richard will have to wear a bag?'

'That's right,' Chrissie said. 'I'm sure Dr Hunter will be along to see you when the histology results are back, but because I'm going off duty now I just wanted to come and see you both.'

'That's kind of you, Dr Paige, thank you,' said Mrs Morton. 'Richard said you'd been very kind to him and we really do appreciate it.'

'Not at all.' Chrissie smiled and briefly touched the woman's shoulder.

As she left the ward Chrissie saw that Alison was at the nurses' station and suddenly, and probably for the first time ever, she felt she wanted to avoid her friend. She simply couldn't face telling her about Sean and what had happened in Theatre. She would have slipped by, hopefully unnoticed, but Alison, it seemed, had other ideas.

'Chrissie!' she called. 'Don't go.'

Chrissie stopped and turned. 'Alison,' she said. 'I'm sorry, I'm very tired. I just want to get home.'

'Yes, I'm sure you do—so would I in your position. Oliver came in and told us the news.'

'News?' Chrissie raised her eyebrows. 'What news?'

'Well, about our new registrar of course.' Alison blinked.

'Oh, that news,' Chrissie tried to sound nonchalant but the sinking feeling that had been in the pit of her stomach every since she'd first heard the news herself seemed to be gaining momentum, threatening to get right out of control, while at the same time a niggling headache seemed to have taken up residence over her right eyebrow.

'What news did you think I meant?' Alison frowned.

'Who knows, around here?' Chrissie shrugged. 'We seem to be the last to be told anything. Now, if you don't mind, Alison, I really must be going…'

'But, Chrissie, did you know—about Sean O'Reagan, I mean?' Alison was beginning to look bewildered.

'What about him?' said Chrissie coolly.

'Well, that he'd applied for reg—the same as you?' When Chrissie remained silent, desperately searching for the right words, something seemed to click into place in Alison's mind. 'You didn't know, did you?' she said softly at last.

Chrissie took a deep breath. 'No, Alison,' she said at last. 'I didn't know. In fact, I would go far as to say I hadn't the remotest idea, and that I was as surprised as you obviously were when I was given the news.'

'Oh, Chrissie!' Alison stared at her, apparently on this occasion lost for words.

'Well, there's nothing I can do about it.' Chrissie shrugged again. 'On the other hand, I don't have to pretend I'm happy about it.'

'So are you saying he never even mentioned it to you, not even when—well, during the weekend...?'

'No.' Chrissie shook her head knowing the tears, albeit tears of anger, were dangerously close now and willing them not to fall. 'Not even then.'

'I don't know what to say,' said Alison at last. 'I really don't.'

'Then best say nothing,' said Chrissie. 'It's my problem and I have to deal with it.'

'Even so...'

'I must go now, Alison.'

'Yes, OK, but you know where I am if you need me.'

She drove home in the same almost zombie-like state that she seemed to have existed in for the best part of the day. Once in the flat she immediately set about collecting up the few items that belonged to Sean and packing them in his bag, and all the while she did so she felt as if her heart were breaking. After the way Alan had treated her she had vowed she would never put herself in such a vulnerable position again, and now this was precisely what had happened. She had disapproved of Alison, with her willingness to launch herself so readily into relationships, and yet wasn't that exactly what she'd just done with Sean? On the strength of one weekend's acquaintance, he'd turned up here at her flat, and because she'd mistakenly assumed he'd come solely to see her, she'd just fallen into his arms. Well, it wouldn't happen again, she was certain of that.

By the time her doorbell rang her anger was simmering again. She had considered leaving his bag in the porch but then had thought better of it, knowing she had to see him face to face.

Smoothing back her hair, she walked slowly out of her flat and down the stairs to the front entrance. She took a deep breath and opened the door. At the sight of him standing on the threshold, looking impossibly handsome in his leather coat and roll-neck sweater, with one arm on the doorframe and a slightly contrite expression on his face, her resolve almost wavered.

'Chrissie?' he said. 'I looked for you at the hospital but Alison said you'd already left.'

'Was that all she said?' Turning away from him, she walked back up the stairs, leaving him to shut the front door and follow her up to the flat.

'She said you weren't happy about what happened today,' he said.

'That's putting it mildly,' she answered flatly, 'but, yes, she's right.'

By this time they'd reached the flat, and as he followed her inside he must have seen his holdall, which she'd placed in full view on the coffee-table. As Chrissie turned to face him he said, 'I can understand that, Chrissie, but listen...' He stepped towards her as if he would have taken her in his arms but she backed away. 'Chrissie?' He frowned.

'What can you understand?' she said coldly.

'I can understand that you were disappointed at not getting the job. I know how important it was to you—how much you wanted it.'

'Oh, really? Is that so?' There was sarcasm in her voice now and she knew it. 'And when you realised how much I wanted it, you thought you'd have a go and see if you could get it—is that right?'

'What?' He stared at her.

'Was that the only reason you wanted it—because you knew how much I wanted it?' she demanded. 'Or was it to further your own career? What was it you said? Oh, yes, that's right—you thought you'd never make it to consultant in your job in Ireland because the two consultants on your team were both younger guys. Then when I, like a fool, told you about the job I was after and that at least one of the consultants on my team was nearing retirement, you thought you'd be in with a chance—is that it?'

'No, Chrissie, no!' he protested. 'It wasn't like that at all.'

'You must have known you'd stand more chance than me,' she retorted angrily.

'I didn't think so.' He shook his head.

'What, a fully qualified registrar against an SHO?' The tone of her voice was scornful now. 'Oh, come on, Sean, I wasn't born yesterday.'

'Chrissie, please, you've got it all wrong—please, let me explain.' She remained silent, her arms hugging her body as she faced him across the room. 'I'd already applied for the job before I met you at the wedding,' he said.

She stared at him incredulously. 'You expect me to believe that?'

'It's the truth, Chrissie—I swear it.' He held up his hands, the gesture defensive.

'So how would you even have known about the job?' she said suspiciously. 'Unless it was me telling you about it?'

'Michael told me,' he said quietly.

'Michael?' Her eyes widened. 'Why would he have done that?'

'He knew that I was getting frustrated in my present position.'

'So when did he tell you?' She still sounded suspicious.

'A few weeks ago when the position was first advertised—he phoned and told me that the post of surgical reg was coming up. I know he's in Orthopaedics but I guess Caitlin must have mentioned what was happening in the surgical department.' He paused. 'Honestly, Chrissie, you must believe me—that's the honest truth.'

She continued to stare at him, desperately wanting to believe him, then her eyes narrowed. 'OK,' she said, 'so you knew about the position because Michael told you, but what I don't and can't understand is why you didn't mention that fact when I told you that I also had applied for the same job.'

'I don't know,' he said humbly. 'I should have done, I know that now, but I guess at the time it was because you seemed so excited about it. I didn't want to dampen your enthusiasm…'

'Knowing that you would get the job over me any time?'

'No!' He shook his head. 'By simply admitting to you that we were in competition. If I remember rightly, Chrissie, the only thing you were really concerned about was competition from outside Ellie's.' He inhaled deeply. 'But, actually, if you want the truth, I really didn't think I stood a chance.'

'Oh, come on.' The note of scorn was back in her voice.

'No, really. When you told me that you'd applied, I thought they would go for someone they knew, someone in their own hospital.'

She was silent again, deliberating over what he had said. Then, lifting her head, she said, 'OK, *if* I accept that, and it's a very big if, what I still can't accept is the way you turned up here, leading me to assume that it was me you'd come to see—'

'But it was,' he interrupted.

'When all the time,' she carried on as if he hadn't spoken, 'you had an ulterior motive for being here, and all the time you were here you still didn't mention your real reason.'

'I didn't see any point,' he said quietly.

'You didn't see any point!' Her voice had risen, was quite shrill, in fact, and she hated herself for allowing that to happen. 'You expect me to understand the fact that you left my bed here this very morning, knowing full well that I was nervous about the results of the interview, we shared breakfast…and…and you even wished me all the best before I left the house…when all along you were also waiting for the result?' She was shaking now.

'Like I said, I still thought I didn't stand a chance—'

'Well, it just shows how wrong you were, doesn't it?' Desperately she tried to pull herself together.

'It could so easily have gone the other way,' he said quietly. 'You could have got the job or, come to that, neither of us might have got it. I understand there were other applicants.'

'So what would you have done if I'd got it?' Chrissie demanded. 'Would you have told me then?'

'Yes. Maybe... I don't know, but listen, Chrissie, please, I'm sorry I didn't tell you, really I am, and I realise now that I should have done. I did try to tell you on a couple of occasions but somehow it had gone too far. Because I hadn't told you at the very beginning, somehow I found it impossible to do so afterwards. And as for me coming here—well, it really was because I wanted to see you again.'

'And because you had an interview to attend,' she retorted bitterly.

'Well, yes, that as well,' he admitted. 'But it was good, wasn't it, Chrissie?' He lowered his head and tried to look into her eyes but she turned her face away. 'Come on, you can't deny that. What we had was good... Chrissie?'

She took a deep breath. 'Yes,' she admitted at last, 'it was good...'

'Well, there you are, then—'

'But it was all based on a lie.'

'I didn't lie to you, Chrissie.'

'It was a lie by omission, Sean. Someone else did that to me once—he omitted to tell me that he already had a wife, and I vowed then that I would never let anything like that ever happen again. I'm sorry, Sean, but I'm not sure I would be able to trust you again.'

'Chrissie!' He looked astounded. 'You can't mean that.'

'I'm sorry, but I do. I told you in Ireland I doubted I was ready to trust anyone again or to start another relationship. Now I know my instincts were right.'

'So where does that leave us?' A bleak expression had come into his eyes.

'There was no "us",' she said briskly. 'Not really. One weekend doesn't constitute a relationship.'

'I thought it was more than that,' he said tightly.

'So did I, at the time.' She shrugged. 'But I was wrong.' She swallowed, wishing he would just go, afraid that if he stayed much longer he would see the tears that were dangerously close to the surface, and if that should happen there was no telling where things might end.

'But we shall have to see each other…work together…'

'Yes,' she agreed. 'You will be senior to me. But that's all there will be, Sean. From now on our relationship will be strictly professional.'

He was silent for a few moments, as if digesting what she had just said, then with a sigh he picked up his bag. 'Well,' he said sadly, 'if there's nothing further I can say to make you change your mind…'

'No, Sean, there isn't,' she said firmly.

'Then I guess I'd better go.' He began to walk towards the door but when he reached it he turned. 'I knew you would be upset with me, Chrissie, but I didn't think you would take it this badly.'

'I'm sorry,' she said tightly, 'but that's the way it is.'

'In that case, I really had better go.' His voice had changed now, was strained. 'I'll see myself out—don't bother to come down.'

She listened to him go down the stairs, then to the sound of the front door as he closed it behind him, before she sank down onto the sofa. And it was only then that she gave way to the tears.

Sean could scarcely believe it. Everything seemed to have been going so well with Chrissie ever since the moment he'd landed up on her doorstep and to his complete and utter surprise she'd almost fallen into his arms. He'd imagined she might have been bewildered by him not telling her about his application for the job, upset even, but because he'd never really considered himself as a serious contender, he'd never looked further than that.

When the board had actually offered him the job his initial delight had been tempered somewhat by anxiety over how Chrissie would react, but given the intimacy they had enjoyed in the last few days he hoped she would be able to handle it. And maybe, once she'd got over her sense of disappointment, she would be only too pleased to have him move to England and hopefully to play a more permanent role in her life.

Nothing, however, had prepared him for the way she had reacted. The way it had happened had been unfortunate to say the least. He'd been hoping to see her alone to break the news about his appointment, but he hadn't seen her, and then Maxwell had invited him to attend Theatre 'to get the feel of the place'.

For Chrissie to have found out in such a way, right there in Theatre with an anaesthetised patient between them, had been bad enough, but what had followed afterward at her flat had been a hundred times worse. She had practically accused him of lying, of making love to her under false pretences, and nothing he had been able to do or say had seemed to make any difference.

By the time he returned to the small hamlet on the outskirts of Franchester and the old farmhouse that Michael and Caitlin were in the process of renovating, it was to find that the pair of them had returned from their honeymoon. After the first greetings and enquiries about their honeymoon in Venice, Michael brought up the inevitable question of Sean's application for the post of registrar at Ellie's.

'Believe it or not, I got the job,' said Sean.

'Oh, well done. Congratulations!' Michael clapped him on the back. 'That's wonderful news, isn't it, Cait?'

'Yes, it is,' Caitlin agreed. 'But you don't sound particularly thrilled about it, Sean,' she observed. As he pulled a face, she added shrewdly, 'It's Chrissie, isn't it?'

'Yes.' He nodded. 'I suppose you could say that.'

'OK,' said Michael with a shrug, 'so she didn't get the job this time, but there will be other times. And surely she's pleased that you got it…isn't she?' he added with a frown when Sean's expression didn't change.

'Not so you'd notice,' Sean replied.

'But isn't she pleased that the pair of you will be working together? I thought you and she…?'

'Yes,' Sean said, 'so did I. But it's not quite as simple as that.'

'So what's the problem?' Caitlin frowned.

'Well, for starters, she didn't know I'd applied for the job. She only found out today, after I'd been appointed.'

'Oh, Sean, for goodness' sake!' Michael almost exploded. 'Why on earth didn't you tell her?'

'I should have done, I know.' Sean looked contrite. 'I should have told her at the beginning but because I didn't it became more and more difficult to do so as time went on. The other thing was, I didn't really think I'd get the job anyway. Maybe if I hadn't got it and Chrissie had, or even if she hadn't and it had gone to someone else, she might have been able to forgive me for not telling her. As it is…' He shrugged helplessly.

'So what happens next?' asked Caitlin.

'I need to go back to Dublin and sort things out—work out my notice and put my flat on the market—then I come back here.'

'Where will you live?' asked Michael. 'Chrissie...?'

'I shouldn't think so.' He pulled a face. 'At least, not the way she's feeling at the moment—but I don't intend giving up.'

'You could stay here for a while if you like,' said Caitlin with a quick glance at Michael.

'That's very kind of you,' Sean replied, 'but, no, I wouldn't dream of it, with the pair of you just married.'

'So what will you do?'

'Maxwell said there's a vacant flat in hospital accommodation at the moment. I think I'll take that for the time being, then later I'll look around for somewhere of my own.'

'It'll be great to have you at Ellie's,' said Michael. 'And, like I told you before, on the team you'll be working with there are much better prospects of a consultancy than where you are in Dublin. Oliver Stark will be coming up for retirement in the not-too-distant future and Maxwell Hunter's not exactly in the first flush of youth. Things are really looking good.'

'Apart from me upsetting Chrissie,' said Sean ruefully.

'Let me talk to Chrissie,' said Caitlin.

'Certainly,' Sean replied, 'if you think it will do any good.'

'Well, it won't do any harm,' Caitlin said firmly.

Chrissie was getting ready for bed when her phone rang. She thought at first it might be Sean and nearly didn't answer it, but when she did she found to her delight it was Caitlin. 'Oh,' she said, 'you're back. How was the honeymoon?'

'Absolutely wonderful,' Caitlin replied. 'I can fully rec-
ommend married life.'

'Ah, well, those are delights I doubt I shall ever know
about,' Chrissie said.

'Now, that I refuse to believe,' said Caitlin lightly, then
went on, 'But on that subject, what is all this we're hear-
ing about you and Sean?'

'I think that's a subject I prefer not to talk about,' said
Chrissie tersely. 'I know he's now your brother-in-law and
all that, but at the moment it's a very sore point.'

'Well, I'm sorry you didn't get the job, Chrissie, I really am.'

'Did you know Sean had applied for it?' asked Chrissie
curiously.

'No, I didn't, as it happens,' Caitlin replied. 'At least,
not until we were in Venice when Michael happened to
mention it, and that was after Sean had phoned and asked
for your phone number. He was very keen to get in touch
with you again, Chrissie.'

'Yes, I bet he was.'

'I think you've got it all wrong where Sean is concerned.'

'No, I don't think I have. He tricked me. He led me to
believe that he'd come to England purely to see me, when
all the time he'd come for an interview for the very job that
he knew I wanted so badly.'

'But, Chrissie—'

'No. We spent the whole weekend together because I
thought he was there simply for me. And he still didn't tell
me the real reason he was here. In the end I found out in
the worst possible way, after I'd learnt I hadn't got the job
and during an operation. He swanned into Theatre with

Maxwell Hunter and I was told in front of the whole team that he was to be the new registrar.'

'That's terrible,' Caitlin admitted. 'But, Chrissie, he really does care for you.'

'Then he has a funny way of showing it. No, Caitlin, I'm sorry, but for me it was shades of Alan Peterson all over again and quite simply I'm not prepared to put myself through anything like that ever again. I've come to the conclusion that I'm better off without a man in my life and the way I'm feeling right now I don't think there's anything or anyone that can make me change my mind.'

CHAPTER EIGHT

DURING the two weeks before Sean took up his new position as surgical registrar at Ellie's, Chrissie found herself experiencing a whole range of emotions. Anger was still present for the way in which she thought he had tricked her, together with deep disappointment at not being offered the position herself, but as time went on another emotion crept in, one which surprised and rather dismayed her. To her annoyance she found that she missed him because what he had said to her before he had left was indeed true—it had been very good between them, and deep down, given the right circumstances, Chrissie suspected it could have been even better.

But it was over now, so there was no way she would ever know. There was no going back because to do so would have simply made her look foolish. She'd made her decision and made it perfectly clear to Sean that anything that might have been between them was over, and that in the future any relationship would be purely on a professional level.

But there were times, she was forced to admit, when she wished it were otherwise, times such as in the middle of the night when she would wake and think for one wild exciting moment that he was there beside her, that he would reach out for her again and make love to her with an intensity that would almost drive her out of her mind. Then in the cold light of day she would dismiss such fanciful notions, knowing that if she couldn't trust him, it was useless to travel any further down that particular road. She'd done that once before, given her all to a man who had been less than honest with her, and it had almost destroyed her. Never could she let that happen again.

Alison thought she was mad, and went on and on at her to try to make her change her mind. 'Men like that don't come along too often in a lifetime,' she ranted on one occasion.

'Just as well,' Chrissie had retorted.

'OK, so he omitted to tell you something—is that so terrible? I just wish Liam would come over to see me. I wouldn't care if there were a whole raft of things he chose not to tell me.'

'Like the fact that he thinks nothing of luring a girl into bed then moving on to the next one?' she'd snapped back. The moment she'd said it she wished she could have bitten out her tongue, but it was too late. The damage was done and Alison's stricken expression was to haunt her for days.

In the end the pair of them had come to the conclusion that the best thing they could do was to write off both Irishmen. But for Chrissie that, she knew, was going to be easier said than done, given that Sean was coming back to England and would in effect be her senior at work. For Alison it might be simpler, knowing that she might never have to set eyes on Liam again.

As the days passed Chrissie found her emotions torn between excited anticipation on the one hand and dread at seeing Sean again on the other.

At the hospital it was confirmed that Richard's tumour had indeed been malignant and after he'd recovered from the surgery, he was scheduled for a course of radiotherapy.

'We go on fighting,' he said to Chrissie. 'I'm determined to give my daughter away when she gets married next year.'

'And you will,' said Chrissie firmly. 'There's no question about that.'

As the days passed she found her nervous tension mounting steadily, even more so because she didn't know the exact date that Sean was due to take up his new post. She decided that what she really needed to do was to find out from someone so that he wouldn't once again have the advantage over her and take her by surprise. Her opportunity came when she was leaving Theatre one day and Oliver fell into step beside her.

'How's it going, Chrissie?' he asked her, 'You've been looking a little tired lately—I hope we haven't been working you too hard.'

'No not at all, Oliver.' She smiled at him. 'I'm fine.'

'I really am sorry you didn't make registrar this time,' he said, and she knew he meant it. 'If it had been simply down to me…'

'I know, Oliver. But it's OK, really it is.'

'Maybe so, but you must be disappointed.'

'Well, yes, but I guess that's life, and hopefully there will be other opportunities.'

'Oh, undoubtedly,' he agreed. By this time they had almost reached the ward and Chrissie decided to use those last few moments to her advantage.

'Speaking of the new surgical registrar, do you have any idea when we can expect the pleasure of his company?' She spoke lightly, casually, but for some reason her heart had started to thump rather loudly.

'Next week, as far as I know,' Oliver replied.

'I see,' she replied. 'Just so I'm prepared.'

So she had a few more days to steel herself and her emotions so that they wouldn't let her down when once again she would have to come face to face with Sean.

Sean missed Chrissie—there were no two ways about it. He missed her smile, he missed the way her hair would swing lightly and brush her shoulders, he missed everything about her. He wanted to phone her, to talk to her, to try once again to explain why he had acted in the way he had, to make her understand that it had never been his intention to trick her or upset her in any way. He cared about her too much for that, but because of what had happened he knew he would have to tread very carefully in the future.

He couldn't wait to get back to England to take up his new position, settle into his hospital accommodation— albeit temporary—and perhaps then he could gradually try to persuade Chrissie how much he cared for her. He knew there was no point in trying to rush her. She had made it perfectly plain to him that not only was she disappointed at being passed over for him but that she was also convinced that he had tricked her into sleeping with him.

Gradually, in the time it took him to tie up his affairs in Dublin, he reached the conclusion that the best way he could hope to win Chrissie back was to play things really cool between them—at least to start with. If that approach didn't work, maybe he would have to think again. Perhaps then a more masterful approach would be called for—the very thought of that sent his pulse racing—but he knew caution would have to be the keyword if Chrissie wasn't to think he was simply trying to trick her into bed again.

On the Monday morning after her talk with Oliver, Chrissie woke up and got ready for work in a frenzy of anxiety. She imagined that by now Sean would have arrived and settled himself into his flat in the large old house behind Ellie's that the doctors used as accommodation. It already felt strange knowing that he was only a couple of miles away, instead of comfortably out of harm's reach in Dublin.

She drove to work then sat for a moment in the car park, desperately trying to get herself under control. The only way to play this, she told herself firmly, was to play it cool—pretend to him that he didn't matter to her in the least, and the fact that they were going to have to work together for the foreseeable future was of very little consequence. If only it were true, she thought as at last she stepped out of her car. Taking a deep breath, she lifted the collar of her coat against the cold wind and made her way into the main building.

The first person she saw on reaching the ward was Alison and any thoughts she might have had about keeping the new registrar's arrival completely low-key were quickly thrown to the winds.

'He's here!' said Alison, her eyes glittering dangerously. 'Have you seen him?'

'Er...who?' Chrissie raised her eyebrows innocently.

'Hah!' said Alison derisively. 'You can't play that don't-care line with me, Chrissie Paige. You may be able to fool the others, but not me.'

'OK.' Chrissie's shoulders slumped a little. 'I give in. No, I haven't seen him.'

With a quick, almost furtive glance over her shoulder, Alison went on, 'He came up here about ten minutes ago, had a good look around, tried out his charm on everyone— you know, all the usual blarney—then he was gone. It was my guess he was looking for you.'

'Don't be stupid,' snapped Chrissie. 'I told you, I made it quite plain to him before he went back to Ireland that from now on—'

'Yeah, I know—and you think that'll stop him?'

'Well, it had better,' said Chrissie coolly, 'because he can try all the Irish charm he likes but it won't cut any ice with me.'

Caitlin was the next one. 'Hello, Chrissie,' she said coming out of her office a little later. 'Have you seen Sean yet?'

'No, Caitlin, I haven't.' This time she managed a weary, almost nonchalant note in her voice but she was quick to notice Caitlin's reaction—one of hurt surprise—and she almost regretted her response.

'Well, he moved into his flat at the weekend and he's really going in at the deep end here this morning—we have a full theatre list.'

'It was what he wanted,' Chrissie said coolly.

'Well, yes, quite,' Caitlin replied, then almost as if she realised she needed to change the subject she said, 'Chrissie, while you're here, could you have a word with a woman who is for surgery this morning? She's rather agitated. Oh, and Melanie Ross is in again.'

'Transplant this time?' Chrissie looked up quickly, relieved to be able to focus on something else.

'We are hoping so,' Caitlin replied. Perhaps you'd have a word with her as well.'

'Of course I will.' Chrissie nodded and, draping her stethoscope round her neck, she strode purposefully onto the ward, thankful that at last she had something to focus on other than the fact that Sean might appear at any moment.

Melanie Ross was a young woman of twenty who over the years had seen rather more of the inside of Ellie's than she would probably have wished. She had a history of kidney disease and had spent a large proportion of her teenage years undergoing dialysis. It had now reached the stage where a kidney transplant was the only way forward. Testing had revealed that the girl's mother, Jane, was a perfect match, and in the last few weeks Oliver had been waiting for conditions to be right for both Melanie and Jane in terms of the presence of infection, blood-pressure control and temperature before he carried out the transplant.

Chrissie stopped at the foot of Melanie's bed and as the girl looked up from the book she was reading Chrissie smiled. 'Hello, Melanie.'

'Hello, Dr Paige. Have you heard? Sister says we're almost ready for the off.' The girl's face was bloated from all the drugs she had been receiving but her eyes were as bright as ever.

'I know.' Chrissie perched on the edge of the bed. 'It's brilliant news, isn't it?'

'Yes, they're going to admit Mum tomorrow, and if all goes well the op will be in a few days' time. Just as long as I don't go and get a cold or something. We've been at this point before, haven't we?'

'Yes, Melanie,' Chrissie agreed, 'we have. But I have a feeling this is it.'

Melanie lowered her voice. 'Have you seen the new doctor?'

'What doctor would that be?' Chrissie was studying Melanie's chart and didn't look up.

'Not sure who he was. He came in here a little while ago with Sister and had a look around. I think he's Irish, like Sister—at least, his accent sounded the same as hers. He was dead good-looking—I hope he's here to stay. Perhaps he'll do my operation.'

'I thought you wanted me to do your operation,' said Chrissie, standing up and replacing Melanie's chart on the bed rail.

'Oh, I do,' Melanie said swiftly, 'but you wouldn't be able to do all of it, would you, Chrissie? You told me once before…'

'That's quite right,' Chrissie agreed. 'I can only assist at present.'

'Well, maybe you could assist him.'

'I imagine it will be Dr Stark who performs your transplant, Melanie.'

'Oh, yes, of course, I was forgetting,' said Melanie. 'I like Dr Stark, but…well, I have to say, I wouldn't mind this new guy putting me to sleep.'

Leaving Melanie to her book, Chrissie moved on to the second patient that Caitlin had asked her to see. For some reason her conversation with Melanie had left her feeling faintly irritated—not with Melanie herself, heaven forbid, the poor girl didn't need anyone getting irritated with her at this stage of the game—but rather with the girl's reaction to Sean. Was there nowhere the man hadn't been that morning? It wasn't as if she was late, but it seemed he had been everywhere before her and had spoken to everyone. And, as she had rather suspected would be the case, his Irish charm had left a devastating impression in its wake. Well, they were all welcome to it, welcome to him, she told herself fiercely. They didn't know him like she did, didn't know how he could sweet-talk anyone into believing anything, how he could trick a girl into his bed by allowing her to think she was the most important person in his life, his reason for living...when all the time...

And they didn't know what it felt like to be in his arms, to feel his hands tangled in her hair, his lips on hers gently exploring...they didn't know what it felt like to have him make love, to lift her to a place she had only dreamed of...they didn't know...

'Dr Paige, are you all right?'

Chrissie jerked her head up to find two care support workers, who had obviously come onto the ward to start their bed-changing routine, standing before her and staring at her in consternation.

'What?' she said in bewilderment. So lost in her thoughts of Sean had she become that she had been totally unaware of those around her.

'You looked so out of it,' said one of the women. 'We thought there was something wrong.'

'No, no, not at all,' said Chrissie briskly, desperately attempting to pull herself together. 'I'm fine, thanks. Now, I have another patient to see.' Looking around at the other beds in the six-bedded bay, her eye fell on Ruth Ashfield. 'Ah,' she said, moving towards the bed. 'Mrs Ashfield, hello, I'm Dr Paige. I thought we'd have a little chat about your operation.'

For the next ten minutes Chrissie talked to Ruth, who was to have a lumpectomy that day on her left breast. Needless to say, she was very nervous and fearful, both about the operation and what might follow, and Chrissie hoped she was able to at least partly allay some of those fears.

'Will you be in Theatre?' asked Ruth as Chrissie prepared to leave.

'Yes, I think I will. As far as I know, I shall be assisting Dr Stark today.' She didn't say that there could well be changes that day, that the schedules might have to be adapted to accommodate the fact that they had a new surgical registrar.

She was on edge all day, thinking she heard Sean's voice, thinking he might appear at any moment in the scrub room, in Recovery, Theatre itself. But he didn't, and when towards the end of the day when she finally heard that he had been operating in day theatre and not the general theatres, her nerves were in shreds.

And then, as so often happened in those situations, when she finally relaxed a little, he was suddenly there before her and her heart turned over.

It was right at the end of the day, just before she went off duty, and she was behind the desk at the nurses' station on the surgical ward. Alison was there, as was Caitlin, and as Sean strode onto the ward and stopped at the desk, Chrissie felt her mouth go dry.

'Chrissie.' He nodded briefly.

'Sean.' Her reply, she hoped, was equally cool but suddenly she was only too aware that both her friends were watching, trying to gauge the reactions as she and Sean met again. She lowered her gaze from his and went on sorting the pile of patient records, which she had been doing before he'd appeared. She thought he was going to say something further, ask how she was or maybe make some comment about his first day, but instead he turned to Caitlin.

'Just two overnight patients for you, Sister, from day surgery,' he said briskly. 'Gordon Evans, whose blood pressure is very low, and Edith Janes, who had difficulty coming round after the anaesthetic.'

'Thanks, Sean,' said Caitlin softly, then, loud enough for others to hear, she said, 'So how has it gone—your first day in surgery?'

'Pretty well.' He gave a faint smile, nothing like his usual charismatic one. 'One theatre is much like another, you know.'

'Yes,' Caitlin agreed, 'I dare say it is. What about your flat—is that OK?'

'It'll do.' Sean gave a grimace. 'Pretty basic, but it will have to do until I can find something better.' He paused. 'I'll just go and check on those two patients, then I'll be away—it's been a long day.' With that he turned and, without so much as a glance in Chrissie's direction, walked off into the ward.

Chrissie swallowed and put her head down even lower. This was what she'd wanted, wasn't it? A working relationship between them that was strictly professional. She'd said that, had made it quite plain, in fact, that there was to be nothing further between them, so if that was the case, why now did she feel as if she'd been hit by a sledgehammer, a blow that had sent her reeling and left her feeling empty and utterly miserable? It was what she wanted, wasn't it, for heaven's sake, so what was wrong with her?

If she was honest, she knew what was wrong. She had imagined that when they did actually meet again he might have been a bit cool to start with but that the old easy charm would be there lurking just below the surface, that the amusement would still be there in those devastating blue eyes, but it hadn't been like that at all. Not only had he been cool, after that first terse hello he'd practically ignored her while the expression in those blue eyes, far from conveying amusement, had been positively bleak. She hadn't thought it would be like that. It was dreadful, and it had cut her to the quick. She found herself hoping that the others hadn't noticed anything untoward and although Caitlin bustled away to receive her new patients, predictably it was Alison who hovered.

'You all right, Chris?' she asked, casting a sidelong glance at her friend as she bent over the desk.

'Yes, I'm fine.' Chrissie nodded.

'You don't look fine,' said Alison bluntly, 'and let's face it, he was a bit off with you, wasn't he?'

Chrissie shrugged. 'It was what I expected,' she said tersely. 'I told him that was how it was going to be from now on.'

'Yes, I know, but I still think he could have been a bit more friendly towards you. I mean, when you think of it, it was only just over a couple of weeks ago when the pair of you were—'

'Yes, I know, Alison.' Chrissie interrupted her friend before she could go into graphic detail, then with a deep sigh said, 'You don't have to remind me. But that's all over now. It's in the past and it's time to move on.'

'OK.' Alison shrugged. 'I didn't mean anything by it, I was only trying to—'

'Yes, I know.' Chrissie's voice softened.

'I've been worried about you,' Alison went on. 'You haven't been yourself lately.'

'Well, don't be. I'm fine, really I am.' She paused and glanced at Alison. 'And while we're on this subject, what about you?'

'Me? What do you mean?'

'Liam?'

'Who?' Alison raised questioning eyebrows.

Chrissie allowed herself a chuckle in spite of her misery. 'OK,' she said. 'Point taken.'

Sean decided, as he made his way back to the rather bleak little flat that had been allocated to him, that the moment at the nurses' station when he and Chrissie had come face to face for the first time since his arrival at Ellie's had arguably been one of the worst moments of his life. All day, ever since he'd arrived at the hospital, he'd been in a frenzy of anticipation at seeing Chrissie again, so much so that he'd seriously begun to doubt whether or not he would be able to keep to his earlier resolve and give the at least outward appearance of being cool and impartial. He'd imagined he'd be working in general theatre, possibly with Maxwell, but he'd found that the consultant had decided to take annual leave and that he and Mustapha Ibrahim, the other surgical registrar, were to operate in the day surgery unit. This meant that, because Chrissie was on the main surgical unit and in Theatre, assisting Oliver Stark, he didn't set eyes on her until late in the day.

She'd been standing at the desk at the nurses' station,

together with Caitlin and that staff nurse, her friend Alison. They'd all looked up as he'd approached the desk but he'd only had eyes for Chrissie. She'd obviously come straight from Theatre because she'd still been wearing her theatre greens and had had her hair tucked into a blue and white theatre cap. There had been something vulnerable about the exposed nape of her neck, and he'd had to fight to get his emotions under control and remind himself fiercely that coolness was the keyword. He'd known that if she'd thought for one moment that he was using their recent intimacy or treating her in any way that was overly familiar then he was sunk for ever.

'Chrissie.' He nodded slightly as he said her name, but his voice had sounded strained even to himself, not like his voice at all.

'Sean.' His name on her lips sounded just as strained but briefly as her gaze met his he thought her stony expression must surely melt a little. But no. Far from melting, she averted her gaze and carried on with something she had been doing on the desk. For one moment he was stunned: he hadn't quite expected that. Coolness, yes, maybe, but this indifference? Was this the same woman who'd made love to him with such sweetness, with such passion? He felt his stomach lurch, then mercifully Caitlin spoke and he was forced to concentrate on what she was saying in order not to make a complete and utter fool of himself.

And by the time he left the nurses' station in order to visit a couple of patients who'd been on that day's list for surgery, Chrissie still hadn't looked up. It was as if he hadn't been there, as if she'd been totally oblivious to him, while he, in spite of all his plans, had found himself yearning for some little sign from her—a smile maybe, or perhaps just a glance from beneath her eyelashes—but there had been nothing.

Later, as he prepared a solitary meal for himself, he gradually came to realise that there was a distinct possibility that Chrissie really had meant it when she'd said there was no longer anything between them. He knew then that if he was to win her back again, it was going to be an even harder task than he had first envisaged.

CHAPTER NINE

'SO TODAY'S the day, Melanie.' Chrissie stood at Melanie Ross's bedside and looked down at her.

'Yes, it is.' The girl's voice was a mixture of apprehension and excitement.

'Where's your mum?' asked Chrissie, looking towards the bed next to Melanie's, which was empty.

'She's in the bathroom,' Melanie replied.

'How are you feeling?' Chrissie glanced at the girl's chart, which showed regular observations of temperature, pulse rate, blood pressure and fluid output.

'I'm OK,' Melanie said. 'Scared, but OK.'

'It's inevitable that you'll be frightened,' said Chrissie gently, 'but you must look ahead. Just think how marvellous it will be to be free from all the dialysis and all those drugs.'

'But supposing it goes wrong...'

'It's not going to go wrong. You'll soon be up and about and out of here, with the rest of your life in front of you.'

'I didn't mean me,' said Melanie quietly.

'You mean for your mum?' Chrissie frowned.

'Yes.' Melanie breathed a huge sigh. 'You see, all along, over the years, all the concern has been for me—that I have dodgy kidneys, I need dialysis, I might die. But now it isn't only me, is it? Now there's Mum to be worried about as well.'

'There's no reason to be unduly concerned about your mum,' said Chrissie firmly. 'She's fit and healthy—'

'Yes, I know,' Melanie interrupted her. 'Dr Stark has been through all that with me and I know what he says makes sense, but in the night I started thinking… If anything happened to me—oh, I don't doubt Mum and Dad and my brother Thomas would be pretty upset for a while but presumably they'd get over it in time. But what if something happened to Mum? I can't imagine Dad and Thomas without Mum.'

'Melanie, you mustn't upset yourself like this,' said Chrissie, drawing up a chair and sitting beside the girl while all around them the busy morning ward routine carried on. 'Nothing is going to happen either to you or to your mum.'

'There's a risk.' Melanie shook her head. 'You can't pretend there isn't.'

'Any operation carries an element of risk,' Chrissie agreed, 'but the odds of anything going wrong are very, very slender, so you must keep a positive attitude. Everything will be fine—you'll see. I guarantee I'll be back in here tomorrow morning, talking to both you and your mum. And if it makes you feel any better, I've just seen the theatre team, and not only do you have me assisting Dr Stark but that new Irish registrar you liked so much is on the team as well. We'll be doing your op and another team will carry out your mum's surgery.'

Jane returned from the bathroom at that moment and no further mention was made of Melanie's fears. Just moments later Alison appeared, bearing a kidney dish and syringes to give both patients their pre-med injections.

'That gorgeous Irishman is going to help with my op,' said Melanie with a little sigh.

'Well, lucky old you,' called her mother from the adjoining bed. 'On the other hand, that Egyptian doctor who came to see me last night was rather nice, too.'

'That'll be Mustapha Ibrahim, one of our registrars,' said Alison. 'And, yes, he is nice.'

'Not as nice as the Irishman,' said Melanie. 'Isn't that right, Dr Paige?'

Chrissie didn't answer, and as she floundered for a suitable reply Alison came to the rescue, 'I think you'll find Dr Paige is allergic to Irishmen at the moment,' she said with a short laugh, then on a slightly bitter note, added, 'In fact, you could say we both are.'

'Oh, dear,' said Jane, looking up with sudden interest. 'That sounds a bit ominous.'

'No, not really.' Alison sighed theatrically. 'We just put it all down to experience.'

'Is neither of you married?' Jane looked from one to another and when they both shook their heads she said, 'I don't know what's wrong with all the young doctors in this hospital—two lovely ladies like you.'

'Try telling them that,' said Alison, then turned her attention once more to the job in hand. 'Now, ladies, I want you both to lie down now and rest. No more getting out of bed, because you might feel woozy from the effects of the pre-med.'

'I'm going to go down to Theatre and get scrubbed up,' said Chrissie. 'I'll see you down there, Melanie—and, Jane, I'll see you later.' With a nod and an encouraging smile to both patients Chrissie left the ward and made her way down the corridor to the main theatres.

She had just started scrubbing up when she was aware that Sean had come into the scrub room. She didn't see him, simply heard the soft tones of his voice and his accent, which as ever made her go weak at the knees. There was still that coolness between them, which was so at odds with the way they had once been towards one another. But, as much as it hurt, Chrissie now could not imagine it ever being any other way.

'Good morning, Chrissie,' he said as he began the thorough cleansing procedure that took place before any form of surgery.

'Good morning, Sean,' she replied, without looking up.

'I understand you are to assist me this morning,' he said after a moment.

She stiffened slightly. This was not what she had been given to understand. 'I understood I would be assisting Oliver,' she replied.

'Oliver has given this one to me,' Sean said lightly. 'He is to be overall surgical co-ordinator, together with the consultant nephrologist. We are to operate on Melanie, the recipient, and Mustapha and his team on the donor.' He paused and rinsed the soap from his hands and arms. 'Are you happy with that arrangement?' he asked.

'Yes, I suppose so.' Chrissie nodded as she watched the water swirl away down the drain. The arrangement was all right inasmuch as she couldn't do anything about it, but she couldn't help but reflect that if she had got the registrar's post instead of Sean, it might have been her now preparing to carry out what would have been her first transplant. On the other hand, even if that had been the case, she doubted Oliver would have let her do this. Reluctantly she was forced to admit that Sean really did have the edge over her when it came to experience.

'I promised Melanie I'd go into the anaesthetic room,' she said briefly.

'OK.'

'I think…' She hesitated.

'Yes?' he said.

'I think she was hoping you would do the same.'

'Oh, right,' he said. Together they made their way to the anaesthetic room where Melanie, already drowsy from the pre-med, was waiting to be anaesthetised.

'Hello, Chrissie,' she murmured. Looking beyond her, she added, 'I see you've brought that lovely Irishman to see me and that's nice, but…really, I have to say, I still wish it was you doing my op.'

Chrissie was aware of Sean's embarrassment and for a moment was glad of it, thinking it served him right for swanning into Ellie's and taking over a job that should have gone to her, then almost immediately she hated herself for being so childish. What was wrong with her, for heaven's sake? Here she was, a highly trained professional about to take part in an extremely serious and delicate procedure, and she was more concerned with scoring points against her colleague. It had to stop. She had been the one after all to stipulate that their relationship had to be strictly professional, and now here she was being less than professional.

After Sean had had a word of reassurance to Melanie, Chrissie watched as anaesthetist Mark Jepson administered the anaesthetic and Melanie was finally wheeled into Theatre.

The two operations were to be carried out simultaneously and as Chrissie waited for Sean to make the incision—a diagonal cut on the right-hand side of Melanie's abdomen just below her navel—she knew that the same procedure was being carried out on Jane in the adjoining theatre.

Eventually the donated kidney was transferred from the donor to the recipient, and with Chrissie's help the blood supply was connected and the ureter attached to Melanie's bladder. 'Her own kidneys we leave in place,' explained Sean for the benefit of a student who was attending the operation.

Throughout the entire operation, which took around two and a half hours, Chrissie became very aware of Sean's presence, not this time for any petty point-scoring reason or in a sexual way, which might once have been the case, but rather in a deep acknowledgement of the man's expertise as a surgeon and the infinite care he bestowed upon his patient, respecting, as he did, her dignity at every stage of the procedure. Chrissie found herself watching his hands as he carried out the necessary delicate work, admiring their strength and skill, waiting until he requested her help but then only too eager to participate in and to be a part of this life-saving operation.

By the end of the entire procedure the received kidney was already functioning.

'Well done, Dr O'Reagan,' said Oliver with a satisfied nod.

Sean half turned to Chrissie. 'If you would close, please, Dr Paige,' he said, and briefly, very briefly, over the tops of their masks his eyes met hers.

So immersed had she become in what had been and what was happening that just for a moment Chrissie had forgotten the heartache that existed between them and it was as if they were still close. She held his gaze for a long moment, then she murmured, 'Of course.' And looked away.

It was killing him. There were no two ways about it: this coolness between the two of them was almost more than he could bear, because deep down he knew that things could be and should be so very different. That day had been a prime example. He had been quietly pleased when Oliver had asked him to perform the transplant surgery on Melanie, although he had experienced severe reservations when he'd learnt that Chrissie was to assist him. To his mind that was tantamount to rubbing her nose in the fact that he'd got the job of registrar and not her.

When he'd voiced his fears to Oliver, the senior surgeon had dismissed them. 'I think you'll find Chrissie will be fine about it,' he'd said. 'She's a very mature young woman and I'm sure that by now she will have got over any disappointment she may have felt over not getting the job.'

He'd remained unconvinced, however, for even if Chrissie had got over her disappointment, he knew full well she hadn't got over the fact that he'd failed to tell her that he had been an applicant. To make matters even worse, it had been left to him to tell Chrissie that instead of Oliver it was him she would be assisting.

They had been scrubbing up at the time and he'd got the distinct impression she had been less than pleased with the news. She'd looked adorable, with her slender figure encased in her theatre greens and with her lovely long hair tucked up inside her cap, and he had been forced to fight an overwhelming urge to gather her into his arms.

In spite of his misgivings, he felt the transplant had gone well, and he had been taken by the skill and dedication that Chrissie had brought to her work, even though he guessed she must have resented the circumstances. But then there had come a moment right at the end of the operation when he had asked her to close and momentarily her eyes had met his. For once she hadn't immediately looked away, as had become her habit recently, but had held his gaze, so much so that the look in her eyes had almost encouraged him to attempt to end this foolishness between them. He had—in front of the entire theatre team—almost asked her to meet him, have dinner with him, lunch, coffee, anything that might open up the relationship between them again, but she had once again averted her gaze and the moment had been lost.

Now, on reflection, as he showered and washed away the sweat and blood of the last few hours, he was glad he hadn't spoken. If he had, she would undoubtedly have refused him, put him down in front of all their colleagues, and he wasn't at all certain he could have handled that. If it had just been some girl he had been asking for a casual date, it probably wouldn't have mattered—but it wasn't, this was Chrissie, this was different. He'd finally reached the conclusion that she still wasn't ready, that he would have to continue with this cool, softly-softly approach, at least for the foreseeable future, in spite of the fact that doing so was like some incredible form of torture.

He almost admitted as much later that evening when he visited Michael and Caitlin for dinner.

'So it's not going well, then?' said Michael as he refilled Sean's wineglass.

'Not so you'd notice,' said Sean grimly. 'At times it's almost as if I don't exist.'

'Surely she acknowledges you professionally.' Michael frowned.

'Oh, yes, I can't fault her on that,' said Sean, swirling the wine in his glass and watching it run down the sides. 'But that's the problem. It's exactly as she said she wanted it to be—a strictly professional relationship.'

'I've tried,' said Caitlin. 'I really have, but I have to say that does seem all she wants.'

'I could accept that if it wasn't for the time we did spend together. It was just so good...' Sean trailed off, shrugging helplessly.

'We nearly invited her tonight, didn't we, Michael?' Caitlin glanced at her husband, who nodded in agreement.

'She would have thought that contrived if she'd found me here as well,' said Sean.

'That's what we thought,' Caitlin agreed.

'Sometimes I wish we could just start again,' said Sean after a moment. 'Go right back to your wedding day and meet for the very first time. She seemed happy then in that party-type environment.'

'Maybe we should arrange something similar,' said Michael thoughtfully.

'Another wedding?' Caitlin raised her eyebrows.

'No, not another wedding.' Michael grinned. 'I was thinking more on the lines of a party. You know I'm on the social events committee this year? Well, I've been asked to help organise this Seventies Night party at the club. How about you ask Chrissie to come to that, Sean?'

'I could try,' said Sean doubtfully, 'but she might not come.'

'The thing to do is to include someone else at the same time—someone like Alison,' said Caitlin. 'And if that doesn't work, tell her it's for charity—all in a good cause, that sort of thing.'

'And you think getting Chrissie to come to a party will change the way she's feeling?' Sean sounded sceptical.

'Maybe not.' Caitlin shrugged. 'But it's worth a try. After all, you've got nothing to lose and, let's face it, you'd have a much better chance in a relaxed atmosphere with music and dancing than you would anywhere else.'

'Right,' said Sean, 'you're on. Just as long as Chrissie never suspects we've been plotting behind her back.'

Gradually over the next week or so Chrissie grew accustomed to having Sean around. Although the coolness persisted between them, it was a tolerable coolness, but one which nevertheless left her feeling that what had happened to them before was never meant to be. She was glad now that she hadn't allowed herself to become more deeply involved with him than she had, because it had become increasingly obvious to her that what he had told her at their first meeting was absolutely true and that he wasn't ready to settle down. From her own experience she knew that for her that type of relationship needed a level of commitment that Sean simply wasn't able to give. She'd been badly hurt once before, she just wasn't prepared to put herself through that again, and although it hurt her almost every time she set eyes on Sean, speculating on what might have been, she knew that ultimately it was for the best.

On the surgical ward Melanie and Jane Ross both continued to recover satisfactorily from the kidney transplant, then eventually both were discharged. Chrissie happened to be with Alison when Jane's husband arrived to take them home.

'Look after them,' said Chrissie, as David Ross helped his wife and daughter out of the ward.

'I will,' said David. 'It'll be great to have them both home again. Thank you all so much for everything.'

'There's one happy family,' said Alison as they waved them goodbye.

'It's things like that make it all worthwhile,' observed Chrissie.

'Too true,' Alison agreed. As the family paused in the corridor to exchange a word with Sean, who was approaching the ward, she casually added, 'Talking of happy, how are things between you two?'

'Same as ever.' Chrissie shrugged.

'Well, I think it's a shame,' said Alison. 'I thought the two of you made a lovely couple.'

'Leave it, Alison,' said Chrissie warningly.

'All right, I know, but I was simply saying—'

'I know exactly what you were saying—but it just isn't going to happen, so you might as well forget it.'

'I saw him having lunch with that red-haired SHO in Orthopaedics the other day,' said Alison.

To her horror, Chrissie felt her stomach lurch at Alison's words. That particular SHO was notorious for her exploits among the male staff, but Chrissie suspected her reaction would have been the same whoever's name had been linked with Sean's. Which really was quite ridiculous if she thought about it calmly, because sooner or later it was inevitable that Sean would be seen with someone else. She was surprised really that it hadn't happened before.

'You all right, Chrissie?' She realised that Alison was still talking.

'What?' she said. 'Yes, I'm fine.'

'You don't look fine, you look…I don't know, sort of odd.' She paused. 'Does it bother you?' she said.

'Does what bother me?' Chrissie frowned, knowing what Alison meant but wishing she would just let the matter drop, especially as Sean had now left the Ross family and was making his way onto the ward.

'Him seeing someone else,' said Alison.

'Don't be silly,' retorted Chrissie. 'Of course it doesn't. It's a free country—he can see whoever he likes. And it's certainly nothing to do with me.'

'Yeah, right.' Alison sounded less than convinced.

Chrissie would have moved swiftly away before Sean reached them, but he called out and stopped her.

'Just the ladies I wanted to see,' he said. 'For some reason I've been delegated to sell tickets for a Seventies Night at the social club—can I put your names down?'

Chrissie's immediate reaction was to refuse. It was one thing to pretend that all was well between them in a professional situation, but the last thing she wanted was to have to pretend in a social environment. But before she could speak, Alison answered for them both.

'Yes, we'll go, won't we, Chrissie? It's about time we had a night out.'

'Well… I don't know…' Chrissie began.

'Oh, come on,' said Alison, 'it'll do you good. Go on,' she told Sean, 'put us down. Do we have to dress up in flares and frilly shirts?'

'Only if you want to,' Sean replied with a laugh. For one moment he looked utterly carefree and Chrissie's heart missed a beat, because it reminded her just how he had been during that brief time they'd been together. 'We're having a live band,' he went on, 'who apparently will play music from the Seventies.'

'Sounds good fun,' said Alison, 'don't you think, Chrissie?'

'Wonderful,' said Chrissie faintly. For some reason she was unable to look at Sean.

The Seventies Night fell on a Friday and, had Chrissie but known, it was to be the start of a weekend like no other— a weekend that was to have shattering repercussions and which would eventually change her life for ever. At the time, of course, she had no way of knowing anything about that.

She only knew that she faced the evening with a certain amount of trepidation, if not actual dread. What if Sean asked her to dance? How would she respond? Presumably she would have to agree. Then what? How would she cope with being in his arms again—even if it was only in the context of a dance? Would he use the situation to try to sweet-talk her? And if he did, what in the world would she do? Would she be able to hold out against him or would she once again succumb to his irresistible charm as she had before? And if she did, where would that lead? No, she couldn't go down that road again, it only led to trouble and heartbreak. The only answer would be to be strong and resist any such forms of sweet-talking or flattery.

And even as she agonised over such dilemmas, another and somehow altogether more worrying thought struck her—what if he didn't ask her to dance? Supposing he simply ignored her, danced with everyone else but her and ended up with that red-haired woman from Orthopaedics?

How would she feel then? Deep down, she was forced to admit that the prospect of that was somehow infinitely the worse of the two scenarios.

The day started badly for Chrissie. She woke up with a headache and felt vaguely unwell all day. She had a full theatre list and the knowledge that she was also on duty the following day was almost enough to make her pull out of the evening's arrangements.

'Oh, Chrissie, do come,' said Caitlin when she voiced her doubts during a ward round. 'It sounds as if it's going to be fun. Some of the paramedics are going to do a Glam Rock stunt to try to raise even more money.'

'Well, maybe I will,' Chrissie sighed, 'but I think I'll go home and get my head down for a couple of hours first.'

The rest, followed by a leisurely, scented bath, helped to restore her stamina and once she'd dressed in a pair of stonewashed blue jeans and a red, silky top with the thinnest of shoulder straps she was feeling decidedly better. Her hair, freshly washed, she wore loose so that it fell like a soft curtain over her shoulders, and when at last she was ready she slipped on her winter coat before leaving for the hospital.

It was a crisp, cold night, the sky wide and star-studded, which for a moment reminded her of that other night in Ireland, when it had snowed and she and Sean had met for the first time. But she mustn't think about that. This was now and that had been then, this was England and that had been Ireland, and a lot had happened in between.

She knew she was a little late, and by the time she'd driven to Ellie's and parked in the staff car park the Seventies Night in the social club was well under way. She heard the music as soon as she stepped from the car and as the once familiar tunes reverberated in her head, rekindling vague memories of her early childhood, she smiled, pulled her coat more closely around her and headed for the club. In spite of her earlier misgivings, she decided that the evening might not be so bad after all, and where Sean was concerned—well, perhaps she'd be able to keep out of his way, slip into a dark corner somewhere and stay there just enjoying the music.

Any such thoughts, however, were quickly dispelled, for as she emerged from the cloakroom and entered the vast clubroom which tonight had been turned into a dance floor surrounded by tables, the first person she set eyes on was Sean. He in turn had seen her, and even as she watched was purposefully heading towards her across the floor.

CHAPTER TEN

HE SAW Chrissie the moment she entered the club and he breathed a huge sigh of relief. She was late and he had convinced himself that she had decided not to come after all. She looked absolutely gorgeous in a close-fitting pair of blue jeans that showed off her slim figure to perfection, together with a red top in some sort of silky material, which, because of the slenderness of the straps, rendered her shoulders almost bare, allowing her hair to caress her skin in the way he liked.

Immediately he crossed the floor to meet her. 'Chrissie,' he said, staring helplessly at her for all the world like some gauche teenager on his first date. 'I thought...I thought you weren't coming,' he went on lamely.

'Am I late?' She glanced at her wristwatch.

'Er...no, not really.' Sean shook his head. 'Alison was looking for you, so we asked her to join our table...'

'We?' She raised her eyebrows.

'Yes, I'm with Michael and Caitlin—over there.' He indicated a table on the far side of the room. 'You'll join us?' It was more of a statement than a question, not seeming to require an answer, as if it was a foregone conclusion that she would join them. But for one awful moment Sean found himself wondering what he would do if she re-fused—if the coolness between them extended to not even sharing a table. She didn't refuse, however, instead follow-ing him across the floor and taking a seat at the table be-side the others.

'Hi, Chrissie.' Alison grinned at her and the other two called out a greeting.

'What can I get you to drink?' Sean asked, leaning to-wards her and catching the scent of her perfume, which almost sent him into freefall, reminding him of that one wonderful weekend they had spent together.

'Mineral water, please,' she said, glancing up at him.

'Is that all?' He frowned.

'Yes. I'm on duty in the morning. I need to keep a clear head.'

'OK.' He nodded and made his way to the bar. He'd been hoping that a drink would relax her, make her forget the strained atmosphere between them. But there didn't seem any likelihood of that, not if she was on duty the next morning. He'd also been hoping that at least, just for that evening, the casual, almost aloof air that had been main-tained by them both could be dropped. Now it seemed he was going to have to be more careful than he'd thought. She'd seemed a little more friendly towards him but he knew that any false move on his part could put them right back to square one.

While he was on his way back to the table with Chrissie's drink and a second round for the others, the band suddenly struck up with a rock number. With their silver, sparkly costumes, outrageous shoulder-pads and platform boots, the band took everyone's attention. The dancing began, with people taking to the floor in droves as one classic hit made way for another. It was fun, and amidst the laughter Sean watched Chrissie relax, but it wasn't until much later, when the band was taking a well-earned break and the club's resident DJ took over and the tempo slowed right down, that he led her onto the floor and to the slow sensual tones of Barry White drew her into his arms.

It felt like heaven to have her back there where she belonged, to feel the soft, velvety texture of her skin beneath his fingers and the smooth, silky curtain of her hair against his cheek.

'I've missed you, Chrissie,' he murmured, drawing her even closer, so close that he could hear her heart beating against his own.

She didn't answer, didn't agree with him, but then again neither did she attempt to draw away, seemingly content to remain there in the circle of his arms as they swayed gently to the music and the sexy voice of the singer.

And then all too soon it was over, and with a deep sigh of regret he took her hand and led her back to their table, to smiles from Caitlin and Michael and meaningful looks from Alison. But he didn't care—all that mattered was that he had held her again in his arms and she hadn't frozen him out. It was a start.

People were starting to make a move and in sudden desperation Sean turned to Chrissie. 'How are you getting home?' he said softly.

'I have my car,' she replied, 'and I said I'd take Alison home.'

His heart sank. 'I hope,' she went on, 'you weren't thinking of driving me home.'

'Of course not.' He shook his head. 'I thought we might have shared a cab.'

'As I say, there's no need.' She looked up at him. 'But I have enjoyed tonight, Sean,' she said, 'really I have.'

'Yes,' he agreed, then, so that the others couldn't hear, he murmured, 'So have I. Maybe we could repeat it some time?' he added hopefully.

'Maybe,' she said softly, then reached up on tiptoe and kissed him lightly on the cheek. 'Goodnight, Sean.' Then she was gone, together with Alison, out of the club and into the night.

'Well?' said Michael, looking up at Sean.

'Well what?' Sean frowned.

'Was that a success or wasn't it?'

'I would say,' said Caitlin with a knowing little smile, 'that it most definitely was a success. That's the happiest I've seen Chrissie for some time now.'

'Me, too,' Sean agreed.

'So I would say you are in with a chance,' said Michael. 'This time, just make sure you don't do anything to blow it.'

'Don't worry,' said Sean as he pulled on his leather jacket and the three of them headed for the door. 'I certainly have no intention of doing anything like that.'

'Don't you try and tell me there's nothing between you two,' said Alison as she settled down in the passenger seat of Chrissie's car, 'because I simply won't believe it. Not in a million years would I believe it, not after seeing the pair of you together on that dance floor tonight.'

'It was only a dance, for goodness' sake!' said Chrissie.

'Only a dance, she says!' Alison gave a hoot of derision. 'If that wasn't sexual chemistry on show tonight, then I don't know what is.'

'Sexual chemistry? You do talk rubbish at times, you know,' said Chrissie. But there was no animosity in her voice because deep down she was happy. Happy at the way the evening had gone and, in spite of all her earlier resolve to the contrary to keep the relationship strictly professional, happy to have found herself not only in Sean's company again but also in his arms.

'Did you see Her from Orthopaedics?' asked Alison after a moment.

'Yes, I did.' Chrissie nodded. It would have been hard to miss the flamboyant redhead.

'She made a beeline for Sean, didn't she?'

'Yes,' Chrissie said. 'I noticed.'

'I thought she was going to devour him on the dance floor,' muttered Alison. 'I tell you, Chrissie, take it from me, if you want that guy—and who wouldn't?—you need to snap him up fast, because if you don't then sure as hell she will, and if not her then someone else. I've heard on the grapevine there's quite a queue where our dishy new reg is concerned.'

Chrissie felt a deep pang at Alison's words, the sort of pang she'd had when she'd seen the SHO from Orthopaedics dancing with Sean. It felt suspiciously like jealousy.

After she'd dropped Alison off at her flat, Chrissie drove to her own home and parked her car. By the time she got indoors it was to find that her phone was ringing. She knew who it would be before she answered it.

'I just wanted to make sure you got home safely,' Sean said.

'What made you think I might not?' she said lightly, but

deep down she was pleased that he cared and had taken the trouble to call.

'You never can tell these days,' he said. 'You hear such awful things.'

'In Franchester?' she said with a touch of amusement in her voice.

'Anywhere,' he replied firmly.

'Yes, all right. But you needn't worry. I'm home and I'm fine.'

'And you really enjoyed the evening?'

'Yes, I really enjoyed the evening. I said so, didn't I?'

'Yes, you did,' he agreed, 'but I thought you might have just been saying it—you know, being polite and all that.'

'No,' she said firmly. 'I meant it.'

'Good,' he said, 'because I did as well. Like I said, maybe we could do it again some time…?'

'Let's just take things slowly, Sean,' she said, 'and see what happens.'

'OK,' he replied lightly. 'But, Chrissie…?'

'Yes?'

'You're not still angry with me, are you?'

'What about?'

'Me getting the job and not you?'

'I don't think I was ever angry with that. Disappointed maybe, but not angry.'

'But you were angry with me.'

'Yes,' she agreed, 'I was, but it was more because you hadn't told me that you'd applied for the job, and because when you came over for the interview you led me to believe it was me that you'd come to see.'

'But it was,' he protested.

'Amongst other things. But let's not go into all that

again—at least not now. I'm tired, and I need to get some sleep if I'm to go on duty in the morning.'

'So am I forgiven?' he said hopefully.

'Oh, I think so.'

'I didn't mean to upset you, Chrissie,' he said softly, 'and even if I hadn't been coming over for the interview, I would have still come to see you.'

She replied lightly in a noncommittal sort of way, but at his words her hand had tightened round the telephone receiver. Moments later she said goodnight, then hung up.

She slept fitfully that night, her conversation with Sean reverberating in her head, together with the sound of the band as they'd belted out one particular song.

She woke just after six o'clock and in spite of the fact that she had deliberately not touched any alcohol the night before in order to keep a clear head, she felt absolutely wretched. Thinking a shower and a cup of tea might revive her, she prepared for work, only to find that by the time she left the house, if anything, she felt even worse.

During the day she began to feel a little better but a niggle that had started in her head some days before had begun to grow and take on alarming possibilities. At the end of her shift she would have hurried straight home but she was waylaid by Caitlin, who had just come on duty.

'Chrissie,' she said, 'did you enjoy last night?'

'Yes,' Chrissie said, 'it was great. Did you?' she added.

'Oh, yes,' Caitlin replied. 'Michael and I had a wonderful time and I have to say, it was lovely to see you and Sean together.'

'Yes, well…'

'Chrissie…' Caitlin hesitated, clearly uncertain how to proceed. 'Do you think that you and he…?'

'I have no idea. Really, I don't.'

'Well, maybe there's a chance.' Caitlin shrugged hopefully then, looking keenly at Chrissie, she said, 'Are you all right? You look a bit under the weather.'

'I don't feel too brilliant,' Chrissie admitted. 'Too many late nights, I expect. Anyway, I'm off home now.'

She stopped off at the pharmacy on the way home, then in the privacy of her own home she carried out the test that she knew needed to be done.

Sean was on a late shift that day and was grateful for that after the excesses of the night before, but even so he was still finding it difficult to concentrate. All he really wanted was to see Chrissie and convince himself that he hadn't dreamt what had happened, but by the time he went on duty Chrissie's shift must have been coming to an end, and when later he asked Caitlin, it was to be told that Chrissie had gone home.

'Was she OK?' he asked anxiously.

'Well…' Caitlin sounded dubious, which immediately raised his suspicions that once again he'd upset Chrissie in some way.

'She did enjoy last night, didn't she?'

'Oh, yes,' said Caitlin quickly. 'It wasn't anything like that.'

'What, then?' he demanded.

'I don't think she was feeling too good,' said Caitlin.

'Oh?' he said. 'What was wrong?'

'I don't think it was anything much—tiredness probably—but she said she wanted to get home.'

'Do you think I should go round and see her later?' he said.

'Oh, Sean, I don't know.' She stared at him. 'I don't think so. Maybe you should just let things be for the moment. Don't rush her.'

'Yes, OK,' he sighed. 'Patience never was one of my strong points. Things were better last night between us— all I want now is for them to be perfect again.'

'Yes, Sean,' said his sister-in-law gently. 'I know you do. But, like I said, don't rush her. Just take things slowly.'

He had to go into Theatre, where he was performing a bronchoscopy on an elderly man, but as he scrubbed up he found himself worrying over what Caitlin had told him. He hated to think of Chrissie not being well and his first instinct had been to hurry to her side, but at the same time he recognised the sense of what Caitlin had said, and deep down he knew that to rush Chrissie now would be the worst thing he could possibly do. In the end, in order to concentrate fully on the demanding nature of the job in hand, and difficult as it was to do, he was forced to put all thoughts of Chrissie firmly out of his mind.

Chrissie stared at the thin blue line in disbelief as what had until that moment been a niggling possibility became a fact.

She was pregnant.

She sank down onto the bed in shock. She couldn't be. They had been so careful during that one passionate weekend, which, of course, was the only time that it could have happened. There had to be some mistake. The test was wrong.

But a second test taken a few hours later confirmed the first result, so quite obviously there had been a moment when they hadn't been quite as careful as they should have been. Either that or the contraception had failed.

For a moment Chrissie experienced utter despair. This, in all honesty, was the worst possible thing that could have happened. She'd always thought that she would like children one day—but not yet, not at this stage in her life when her career, which she had worked so hard for, had just begun to take off. And as far as Sean was concerned—well, they weren't even in a serious relationship, weren't really in any sort of relationship at all.

Although... When she cast her mind back to that wonderful weekend, which she often did, she had to admit there had been moments when she had imagined what it would be like to be married to Sean and, yes, to have his children. But even then some sixth sense had urged caution, reminding her that Sean himself had told her that he wasn't ready to settle down like his brother Michael, warning her that she shouldn't become too involved with the devastatingly exciting Irishman.

And then, of course, since then it had all changed. Everything now was totally different. For a time they had barely been talking to one another and even now, with some sort of unspoken truce between them, she couldn't imagine his reaction on being told that she was to have his baby.

By midnight she had reached the conclusion that the best thing would be that he shouldn't know, then after a sleepless night, in the cold, cruel light of morning, she doubted there would be a way to prevent him knowing. Round and round her head spun as she tried to get to grips with what had happened.

In the end she recognised that she needed to talk to someone. Her first thought was Caitlin who, with her level-headed calm, would be sure to help her to gain a sense of perspective, but the more she thought about it, she realised that it wouldn't be fair to implicate Caitlin who, when all was said and done, was Sean's sister-in-law. At last she decided the one she would take into her confidence was Alison.

Fortunately, it was Sunday and both she and Alison were off duty. The moment she told her friend she needed to talk to her, Alison said she would come right over.

'What is it?' Alison demanded almost as soon as she set foot in Chrissie's flat.

'I'm pregnant,' said Chrissie bluntly, then promptly burst into tears.

'Oh, is that all?' said Alison with a sigh of relief.

'What do you mean—is that all?' Chrissie stared at her through her tears.

'I thought you were going to say you had cancer or something.'

'No, no, nothing like that.' For one moment Chrissie's perspective shifted slightly. It could have been worse, very much worse, but it still didn't alter the enormity of what was happening.

'Well, you haven't been quite yourself lately...and I thought...' Alison shrugged. 'Anyway,' she stared at her, 'so you're pregnant. I take it Sean is the father?'

'Well, of course he is,' Chrissie retorted indignantly. 'Who else did you think it was, for heaven's sake?'

'Sorry!' Alison grinned. 'But I don't know what you get up to in your spare time, do I?'

'Well, I can assure you, nothing like that,' declared Chrissie firmly.

'Are you certain?' Alison narrowed her eyes.

'Yes. I've done two tests—there's no doubt.'

'Well, congratulations!'

'I'm not sure that's exactly appropriate.' Chrissie sniffed.

'Of course it is. It's great.' Alison paused. 'And does Sean know he's going to be a dad?' she added after a moment.

'Of course he doesn't!' Chrissie stared at Alison. 'This isn't a cause for celebration. It was an accident, something that shouldn't have happened. I imagine Sean would be as horrified as I am.'

'Oh, I don't know,' mused Alison. 'The Irish love their babies and big families and all that sort of thing. I would think he'll be over the moon when he gets used to the idea.'

'I'm not even sure I want him to know,' said Chrissie slowly.

'What?' Alison looked up sharply. 'What do you mean?'

'Exactly what I say. I don't think I want Sean to know about this.'

'What are you saying? You've always been against termination for social reasons…'

'I know.'

'So are you saying that it's different now it's happening to you?'

'No…but… Oh, Alison, I don't know what to do.'

'Right,' said Alison clapping her hands together, 'we need to talk this through—probably over a bottle of wine.' She paused. 'Although, on second thoughts, in your situation maybe a cup of tea would be better.'

If Chrissie had had any doubts over the reality of what was happening, those few words of Alison's brought it firmly home—she shouldn't have a drink because of her condition.

Ten minutes later they sat opposite each other in comfortable armchairs, a pot of tea on the low table in front of them.

'Right,' said Alison, 'first we need to establish a few facts. Number one, you are definitely pregnant.' When Chrissie nodded miserably, she went on. 'Number two, you don't want a termination—is that correct?' Chrissie nodded again. 'In that case, in nine months' time or thereabouts, you will be giving birth. Those are the undisputed facts—right?'

'Of course they are,' muttered Chrissie irritably. 'You don't have to rub it in.'

'I'm not, Chrissie, really I'm not,' Alison protested, 'but now we've got over that, we need to face what options you do have. The way I see it, you have three options.'

'Three?' Chrissie looked up and frowned. 'How do you work that out?'

'Well, first, you tell Sean, and you and he get together and play happy families. All right, all right…' Alison held up her hands defensively when she caught sight of Chrissie's expression. 'Second, you have the baby and bring it up on your own—I'm not sure what you would do about Sean in that situation. I imagine he might notice if you started bringing a buggy into work and depositing a baby in the hospital crèche—and that's always supposing that he hadn't noticed your burgeoning waistline in the months preceding the birth. So, in either of those situations, my guess is you would actually have to tell Sean. I suppose you could always lead him to believe that the baby wasn't his—that you had some secret admirer that none of us knew about. Or failing that, you could tell him the baby is his but that you want to bring it up alone with no involvement with him.'

'And the third option?' asked Chrissie quietly, when Alison had finished.

'What?'

'You said there were three options.'

'Yes, well, third, you have the baby adopted.' She shrugged.

'What?' Chrissie stared at her.

'You could even go away beforehand like they used to do in the old days—only your explanation would have to be a sabbatical, not visiting a maiden aunt at the seaside—and when you came back to work, restored to your former slender self, you could pick up the threads of your life as if nothing had ever happened.'

'Only, of course, it would have happened,' said Chrissie, 'and my life would have changed beyond all recognition because I would have become a mother.'

'Do I take it from that the third option is out?' Alison raised one eyebrow and when Chrissie nodded in reply she said, 'I thought so. I could never imagine in a million years you giving a baby away.' She took a deep breath. 'So,' she said, 'we're left with just two options.' When Chrissie remained silent she said, 'What I want to know is what's so terrible about telling Sean?'

'He'll be horrified,' she said, shaking her head. 'It'll be the last thing he wants.'

'You don't know that for sure,' argued Alison. 'He could well surprise you and be over the moon. And if Friday night was anything to go by, and the way he was looking at you, it could be just what he wants.'

'No.' Emphatically Chrissie shook her head. 'When Michael and Caitlin got married he made it quite plain that there was no way he was ready to settle down—he as good as said that marriage and families were not for him.'

'That was different. It was easy for him to say that

then, it wasn't happening to him. This is, Chrissie, and, let's face it, it's his responsibility as much as yours. He's had his fun and he should be prepared that there could be a price to pay. And actually,' she went on, warming to her theme, 'I have to say, he strikes me as the sort of man who would face up to his responsibilities.'

'Do the decent thing, you mean?' said Chrissie, and there was no disguising the bitter note in her voice.

'Well, not quite like that. I'm sure he'd—'

'I don't want that,' Chrissie interrupted her.

'What do you mean?'

'I don't want Sean to think I've trapped him. I don't want him to feel he has to do the decent thing and marry me for the baby's sake.'

'Hang on a minute—he might want to,' protested Alison.

'Yes, just because there's a baby on the way. No, Alison,' Chrissie cried. 'When I get married I want it to be because a man loves me and not for any other reason.'

There was silence in the room, then Alison gave a long drawn-out sigh. 'OK,' she said at last, 'so that just leaves option two—you have the baby and bring it up alone.'

'Yes,' said Chrissie softly.

'And Sean—what about him?'

'I don't know yet. As you say, it would be impossible to keep it from him entirely, but I don't need to say anything just yet.'

'Maybe not,' Alison agreed dubiously, 'but that day will surely come and probably faster than you think.'

'So I'll deal with it when it does,' Chrissie replied.

CHAPTER ELEVEN

HE COULD scarcely believe it. After all the high promise of the night at the social club, he and Chrissie seemed to be back at square one. He couldn't understand it. He'd taken Caitlin's advice and not rushed or crowded Chrissie in any way, but it seemed to have had an adverse effect and she seemed to be as cool with him as she'd been before the Seventies Night. He even found himself wondering if he'd dreamed dancing with her and holding her close, even the fact that their conversation had seemed to move them on from the almost hostile atmosphere they'd shared ever since he'd taken up his appointment at Ellie's to, if not exactly as they had been during that magical weekend or even as it had been in Ireland, at least something approaching that.

Caitlin had said that Chrissie wasn't too well but had warned him against rushing over to see her. He'd done as his sister-in-law had suggested but now he wished he hadn't listened to her and had gone anyway. Maybe if he'd seen Chrissie immediately after that night in the club she might have been in the same compliant mood and it just might have been easier to let things naturally progress from there.

Now time had put distance between them again and he

was beginning to despair of ever getting back to the way they had once been.

But he was far from giving up. He knew he would simply have to keep on trying to find a way to rekindle her interest in him. Sometimes he felt there was a conspiracy working against him and Chrissie ever getting together again—first Caitlin warning him to show caution, then one morning at work Maxwell informing him that for the following week he would be working in Accident and Emergency.

'They are short-staffed down there,' the consultant told him. 'Two away sick and one on holiday. I agreed to you going, provided it's only for a week. Is that all right with you?'

'I suppose so,' he said. It wasn't all right. It would mean that not only would he and Chrissie be barely talking to each other for the next week, he wouldn't even be working with her either. But he could hardly say that to Maxwell. The surgeon would have taken a very dim view of one of his registrars allowing his private life to encroach on his professional one.

But some good came out of it because it was at that point, after his conversation with the consultant surgeon, that Sean came to a decision. He would work his week in A and E then he would see Chrissie, ask her out somewhere—to dinner maybe, he'd seen a place called Angelo's, a nice little Italian restaurant in town—and ask her once and for all if there was a chance that they could get back to the way they had once been, albeit so briefly. He was sure they could make a go of it. What they had experienced together during that one weekend had been unforgettable and for him, at least, something he had never quite experienced before. He loved her, there was no two ways about it, and he knew he needed to tell her so.

A baby. She was going to have a baby. Chrissie still couldn't quite get her head round the fact. Sometimes she would wake up in the night and the thought would hit her and she would be unable to get back to sleep, or sometimes, on waking in the morning, she would forget for a moment, then the realisation would wash over her and she would lie there gazing up at the ceiling, her thoughts in turmoil. That her life was about to change beyond all recognition she had no doubt, neither was she under any illusion that bringing a baby up on her own would be anything other than difficult. She had even wavered at times and contemplated telling Sean—at least they would be in this thing together then. Although she wasn't really too sure of that. He simply might not want to know, might even—perish the thought—think she'd been with someone else and that the baby wasn't his. Then she could find herself in the rather distasteful area of paternity tests. On the other hand, he might acknowledge the baby as his and decide he had to do the decent thing and stand by her, even marry her. And as she'd told Alison, that somehow was even worse, because he would feel she'd trapped him and deep down she suspected that Sean O'Reagan quite simply wasn't ready to settle down with anyone.

At other times her senses were flooded with sudden feelings of overwhelming tenderness—for the unborn child growing inside her and for Sean and the way things had once been between them. It was at those times that she allowed herself the rare luxury of indulging in thoughts of how things could be. Herself and Sean in a home of their own, preparing for the birth of their baby, and afterwards the three of them living together—Sean and her, caring for the baby. She wondered at length about the sex of the child. Would it be a little girl with fair colouring like her own, or perhaps a boy with Sean's dark hair and deep blue eyes? At such times she usually ended up by dismissing such fanciful thoughts as being the result of raging hormones, and at other times, during bouts of morning sickness or when she'd had to excuse herself from theatre for the umpteenth time to visit the loo, she wished they'd been even more careful during their weekend of passion. But such thoughts didn't usually last too long and for the best part Chrissie found herself regarding her pregnancy with a sense of awe and excitement.

'You should tell him,' Alison stated flatly one day when she called into the flat and found Chrissie pouring over a couple of mother-and-baby books.

'Why?' said Chrissie stubbornly, without looking up.

'Because, as the father, I happen to believe he has a right to know.'

'That doesn't sound like you.' Chrissie looked up in surprise at her friend's unexpected remark.

'Maybe not.' Alison shrugged. 'And to be honest, I didn't even know I felt that way—never really been faced with the situation before. It's easy to pass judgment on hypothetical cases but when you know the people concerned, it's different.'

'What do you mean?' Chrissie frowned.

'Well, you are one of my closest friends and, of course, I care what happens to you, but actually I've grown quite fond of Sean in the time I've known him, and I happen to think he would be very hurt if you don't tell him what's happening.'

'OK!' Chrissie threw up her hands. 'I will tell him.'

'When?' Alison demanded.

'Not just yet. But soon—I promise. Does that satisfy you?'

'I suppose so.' Alison shrugged. 'And what about his reaction?'

'I'll just have to deal with whatever that happens to be at the time,' Chrissie replied with a sigh. 'But whatever it is, I can see that in the end it will be me who will be bringing this baby up so I feel at this point it's up to me to call the shots.'

Alison pulled a face but refrained from further comment.

She missed him. There was no two ways about it. Someone said he was working in A and E, helping out as they were short-staffed, and at the time she hadn't imagined that would affect her. But it did. Almost from the word go she was affected. In Theatre she found herself straining her ears for the sound of his voice and on the wards she was on edge, waiting for him to appear. But, of course, he didn't, because A and E was almost a self-contained unit with its own staffroom and canteen so its staff had very little cause to even set foot in the main hospital.

By the time she left home on Wednesday morning she was counting the days until Sean's return to the surgical unit. She'd told no one how she felt—not Caitlin and certainly not Alison, who would have seized on such a confession and tried to persuade her that if she felt that way then surely it was an indication that the time was right to tell Sean about the baby. That was something she still refused to be rushed over.

It was a calm, still morning with more than a hint of spring in the air. Pale sunshine bathed the countryside, catkins dangled motionless from the trees and in the hedge-rows were the first tell-tale specks of yellow—celandine, or a few early primroses. It was one of those mornings where it felt good to be alive, when winter has felt like a journey in a long dark tunnel and the time has come to emerge into the sunlight, which for Chrissie, with the secret promise of a new life to look forward to, made what happened next even more traumatic than it was.

She was travelling towards the hospital on a straight flat road in a residential area when with no warning a motorcyclist shot out of a turning to her left, right in front of her.

Afterwards, she remembered the feeling of shock, the attempt to apply her brakes intermingled with flashback memories of another road accident in Ireland, then a terrible impact as she collided, first with the motorbike and then, as her car spun out of control, with a brick wall. After that, mercifully, nothing.

She came to in an ambulance with a paramedic bending over her. 'Hello,' he said, 'it's Dr Paige, isn't it?'

'Yes,' she whispered. 'What's happened? Where am I?'

'You were in an accident,' the paramedic replied. 'We're taking you to Ellie's.'

'An accident?' Desperately she tried to remember but her brain seemed to be encased in some sort of fog.

'Yes, a motorbike—do you remember?'

'I don't know...I'm not sure. Am I hurt?' she whispered.

'Not too much, as far as we can see,' the paramedic replied. 'A bit of concussion, and your shoulder...'

'My shoulder...?' Chrissie moved then gave a cry as a shaft of pain sliced through her shoulder.

'Try and keep still,' the paramedic said 'We're nearly at the hospital.'

With a little sigh Chrissie closed her eyes.

It had been a quiet night on A and E and the night staff had just handed over to the day team when word came in of an accident on the outskirts of the town.

'Do we have any details?' asked Charge Nurse Steven Russell.

'A car in collision with a motorbike,' he was told.

'What injuries?' asked Sean, who had just come on duty and was pulling on his white coat.

'The driver of the car was concussed and has a shoulder injury, the motorcyclist suspected internal injuries.'

'Expected time of arrival?'

'Five minutes.'

'Right,' said Sean, 'let's get outside to receive them.'

Moments later the team was assembled in the ambulance bay outside the accident and emergency building.

'Do you know,' observed one of the nurses as they waited, 'that sunshine is really warm this morning.'

'Let's hope it's a sign of things to come,' Sean replied. In the distance the sound of sirens could be heard and when two ambulances swept through the hospital entrance and up the drive, he stepped forward and said, 'Here we go. I'll take the first one. Steven, you take the second.'

The two paramedics jumped from the first ambulance, acknowledged the waiting team with a nod, came round to the rear of the vehicle and opened the doors. Sean stood to one side as the two men lifted the stretcher from the back of the ambulance.

'This is one of our own,' said the paramedic, as he passed Sean. 'One of our doctors from Surgical.'

'What?' Sean swung round, then it seemed that his heart stood still as he realised that the woman on the stretcher was Chrissie.

'Yes,' the paramedic went on, oblivious to the impact on Sean. 'Dr Paige—she's suffered concussion and she has a shoulder injury.' He stopped as Sean took hold of one of Chrissie's hands.

'Chrissie?' he said softly but urgently. She opened her eyes and stared up at him.

'Sean…?' she murmured, 'Oh, Sean, thank God it's you.'

'We'll get you inside,' he said, 'and don't worry, Chrissie, everything is going to be all right.'

As they made their way into a treatment room he demanded, 'Do we know what happened?'

It was one of the paramedics who replied. 'A chap who witnessed it said the motorbike came out of a side road right in front of Dr Paige's car. She didn't have a chance to avoid it. Her car spun round and went into a brick wall.'

The next moments passed swiftly in an assessment of Chrissie and her injuries while the motorcyclist was brought into an adjoining bay for a similar assessment.

'It doesn't look too bad, Chrissie,' said Sean, leaning over her and taking her hand while a nurse checked her pulse and blood pressure. 'We'll need to X-ray that shoulder and we'll keep you under observation for the concussion—'

'Sean,' she whispered, and her grip tightened on his hand.

'Yes,' he said, 'what is it?'

'About that X-ray…'

'Yes, what about it?' He frowned.

'I'll need extra protection,' she said in the same soft tone.

'Extra protection?' He stared at her, not quite understanding what she meant.

'I'm pregnant,' she whispered, 'and my stomach hurts.'

'Chrissie…' He continued to stare at her, for a moment utterly lost for words, then the look in her eyes and the grip on his hand told him all he needed to know. She was indeed pregnant and the baby was his.

'Sean…' Her voice, although low, was urgent. 'I don't want to lose the baby.'

That remark galvanised him into action. 'I want Dr Paige moved to Obstetrics immediately,' he ordered.

'Obstetrics?' The startled nurse stared at him in bewilderment. 'There was nothing about her being pregnant.'

'Well, I can assure you she is,' Sean replied curtly. 'I want her taken up there and put into Tom Fielding's care.'

'What about her X-ray?'

'That can come later—the most important thing for the moment is to save her and her baby.'

From that point on Sean was helpless to do any more for Chrissie as she was moved out of A and E and taken up to the maternity wing. He knew that under senior consultant obstetrician Tom Fielding she would have the best possible care, and that everything would be done to try to save her unborn child.

Her unborn child…his child. He still could hardly believe it. As the porters had wheeled her away he'd briefly taken her hand again. 'I'll come and see you later,' he said, 'and don't worry, Chrissie, everything is going to be all right.'

'Oh, Sean...' she whispered. Then she was gone, whisked away into the lift.

He had no time even to think for no sooner had the lift doors closed and she was gone from his sight than Steven Russell was at his side. 'Sean,' he said, 'Dr Aziz wants you to have a look at the other survivor of the accident.'

'Right.' Sean inhaled deeply then followed the charge nurse back into the treatment room.

The motorcyclist was a young man in his late teens and an assessment of his injuries had shown him to have a suspected broken pelvis and internal bleeding.

'We need to get him to Theatre straight away,' said Sean. 'I'll get scrubbed up.'

Once in Theatre with the patient anaesthetised it was found that the internal bleeding was coming from his spleen, and after further consultation among the theatre team a decision was taken to remove the organ.

For Sean the situation had a bizarre, slightly unreal feeling about it. On the one hand there was Chrissie up there in Obstetrics while they sought to save the life of her unborn child—his unborn child—and here he was being called on to save the life of the young man who had been responsible for the accident that had put Chrissie where she was. He found it took every ounce of his professionalism as doctor and surgeon to concentrate on the job in hand and not be swayed or sidetracked by any personal issues.

At last the operation was successfully over, 'Close, please, Dr Aziz,' Sean said, handing over with a certain degree of relief to the doctor who had assisted him. Tearing off his mask, cap and gloves as he went, he headed swiftly for the shower rooms.

In the shower he gratefully let the water rush over him but his mind was in turmoil. Chrissie was pregnant. He still could hardly believe it. That the child was his he had absolutely no doubt. It must have happened during that one passionate weekend they had shared—he'd thought they'd been careful, had taken adequate precautions, but obviously he was wrong. He was seized with conflicting emotions—awe, disbelief, excitement even, all tinged with a sense of dread that the baby might not survive. His mental calculations told him that it was very early in the pregnancy—one of the worst possible times for a foetus to survive the kind of trauma that Chrissie had been subjected to that day. And if it didn't survive he knew he would be disappointed—no, more than that, he would be gutted.

As he stepped out of the shower and towelled himself vigorously, another thought struck him. Chrissie must have known about this for some time, so why hadn't she told him? Had she known at the time of the Seventies Night at the club when things had seemed so much better between them, or had she only found out afterwards, when that coolness had been back again? There were many questions to be answered but as he dressed then made his way out of A and E and up to Maternity, taking the stairs two at a time, he knew those questions might have to wait because for the time being the only thing of any importance was the well-being of Chrissie and her baby.

He saw Tom Fielding first, in his consulting room. 'How is she?' he asked, coming straight to the point.

'She's had a very lucky escape,' the consultant replied. 'Fortunately, her shoulder isn't broken, just badly bruised.'

'And the baby?' Sean hardly dared ask, knowing the odds in such a situation.

'So far so good,' Tom replied, but as Sean gave a sigh of relief, he cautioned, 'However, it's very early days. Chrissie has suffered some stomach cramps and slight spotting, but an ultrasound showed that all is well with the foetus. I've prescribed a light sedative and a few days' total bed rest and, of course, during that time we'll monitor both her and the baby very carefully. If she gets through these next few days there isn't any reason to suspect she won't have a normal pregnancy and delivery.'

'Thanks, Tom.' The relief on Sean's face must have been only too obvious and Tom threw him a curious glance.

'Tell me,' he said, 'is your interest in this purely professional—one colleague to another—or is it something more?'

Sean hesitated, unsure quite how much he should say, then with a helpless shrug he replied, 'Actually, Tom, it's my baby. Or maybe at this stage I should say I have every reason to believe it's my baby.'

'Well, congratulations!' Tom looked surprised but pleased.

'Thanks.' Sean flushed. 'But the thing is, nothing's been said yet, if you know what I mean, and…well, to be honest, things haven't been too good between Chrissie and me, so I'd appreciate it if you would…'

'Keep quiet?' Tom raised his eyebrows.

'Well, yes.'

'No problem. Mum's the word.' Tom laughed. 'Or maybe I should say dad.' He grew serious again. 'But one thing you have to remember, Sean, is that by now the whole hospital will probably know that Chrissie has been involved in an accident and has been transferred from A and E to Maternity. The grapevine being what it is, it can only be a matter of time before people start drawing their own conclusions.'

'Yes,' Sean agreed ruefully, 'you're right.'

When Chrissie came to it was to find Sean sitting beside her bed and in that instant before the mists cleared from her brain she knew in her heart that he was the only person in the whole world she wanted to be there.

'Sean…?' she said questioningly, and when he took her hand she said, 'The baby?'

'Tom Fielding says you have to rest,' he said softly.

'But the baby?'

'It's all right,' Sean hastened to reassure her, 'but you are to have several days' complete bed rest just to make absolutely certain.'

'I had some pain,' she whispered, 'and some slight bleeding.'

'I know,' he replied gently stroking her hand, 'but it seems to have settled down now and Tom is very optimistic that you should go on to have a perfectly normal pregnancy.'

'What about my shoulder?'

'Not broken apparently, just badly bruised, but, then, if you will have an argument with a brick wall, what else can you expect?'

They were silent for a while and Chrissie was content to simply lie there with Sean beside her, her hand between both of his. Then, as another thought struck her, she turned her head to look at him. 'Sean,' she said, and when he looked up she went on, 'The motorcyclist—is he all right?'

'He has a fractured pelvis,' Sean replied, 'and I had to operate to remove his spleen, which was ruptured.'

'Is he going to be all right?' she said anxiously. Gradually, disturbing details of the accident were beginning to return.

'He was stable when I left him,' Sean replied guardedly.

'Was it touch and go?' Chrissie was starting to feel agitated.

'Let's just say we got him to Theatre in time,' said Sean.

'I could have killed him,' said Chrissie bleakly.

'A witness says he came right out in front of you. You had no chance whatsoever of avoiding him.'

'Maybe so, but I could still have killed him. How old is he?' she suddenly demanded.

'About eighteen, I think,' Sean replied uneasily.

'Eighteen.' Chrissie shook her head. 'His whole life before him and I could have killed him. Just think how I would have felt—it would have been with me for the rest of my life.'

'But it wouldn't have been your fault.'

'Just think, if that had been your son, Sean, and he'd been killed by some woman driving to work…'

For a moment Sean looked stricken then, as Chrissie disentangled her hand from his and placed both her hands over her stomach, he said, 'But he wasn't killed, Chrissie. There's every chance he will make a good recovery. And what you have to remember is that his actions this morning could have caused your death and the death of your baby.'

Chrissie drew in a sharp breath at his words and the tears that had been prickling at the backs of her eyes suddenly brimmed up then trickled down her cheeks. 'I suppose,' she said, dashing the tears away with the back of her hand, 'you want to talk about the baby.'

'Yes,' he said softly. Reaching across to her bedside locker, he took a couple of tissues from a box and handed them to her. 'Yes, of course I do, but not now, Chrissie. Now I want you to rest. I don't want you to get upset about anything. I just want you to rest.'

'All right,' she said. Wiping away her tears and blowing her nose, she rested her head back against her pillows and closed her eyes.

CHAPTER TWELVE

SEAN was in his apartment, killing time before going to see Chrissie, who had gone home that day, when his phone rang. When he answered it he recognised the voice of the caretaker. 'There's someone here to see you, Dr O'Reagan. I found him wandering about in the grounds.'

'Do you know who it is?' Sean asked.

'He says his name is Liam Flynn.'

'Good grief,' said Sean in astonishment. 'You'd better send him up.'

Moments later he opened his door to find a decidedly sheepish-looking Liam standing on the threshold.

'What the hell are you doing here?' Sean stood aside to allow his friend into the room.

'Well that's a fine greeting, I must say,' said Liam with a rueful grin.

'Sorry.' Sean ran one hand over his head. 'I was just so amazed to see you here. What is it, a social visit or…' His eyes narrowed. 'Is there more to it than that?'

'Well, yes, I guess you could say that.' Liam flung himself down onto Sean's sofa with all the familiarity and confidence that only long-term friendship brought.

'Well, come on, then, let's have it.' Sean sat down in the chair opposite.

'It's Alison,' said Liam at last.

'Ah,' said Sean.

'You remember Alison—she was one of Caitlin's friends at the wedding. She and Chrissie—'

'Yes, Liam, I do know who Alison is.'

'What? Oh, yes, I suppose you do. You probably work with her—she's a nurse here as well, isn't she?'

'Yes, Liam, she is,' Sean agreed. He was forced to bite back a sudden surge of amusement.

'Yes, well.' Liam blinked. 'At first I tried to put her out of my mind—you know move on and all that.'

'Like you usually do?' Sean raised one eyebrow.

'Yes, well, you know what it's like. But this time I found I couldn't. I couldn't get her out of my head, Sean— a bit like you and Chrissie, I suppose.' He looked up. 'Speaking of which, how are you and Chrissie?'

'Well, it's a bit of a long story really,' said Sean, 'but let's just say I'm very hopeful that things are going to work out all right. To be honest with you...' he glanced at his watch '...I'm due to go over to her place to see her shortly.'

Liam frowned. 'I would have thought you two would have been living together by now,' he said.

Sean stood up. 'Like I said, it's a long story—I'll tell you all about it some time, but not right now. Besides, I expect you're wanting to see Alison.'

'Actually, I'm a bit worried about that,' admitted Liam.

'Why's that?' Sean frowned.

'I haven't been in touch with her, like I promised I would, and I'm not at all sure that she's going to be pleased to see me.'

'Oh, I don't think you need have too many fears on that score,' said Sean with a short laugh. 'If you come out of here with me now, I'll show you which ward she's on—you'll just about time it right to catch her as she comes off duty.'

'And you think she'll be pleased?' Liam still sounded apprehensive.

'Well, there's only one way to find out,' Sean told him.

It was bliss to be home. Tom had finally given her the all-clear and had allowed her to go on the strict understanding that she was still to rest as much as she could. 'I know you live alone,' he said, 'and that's not easy, but there are people who want to help, Chrissie, and you must let them.'

She knew he meant Sean, just as she knew that she could no longer delay talking to Sean about the baby and the future.

He arrived later that same day and they sat together in the window of her sitting room, which overlooked the river. He looked as handsome as ever in a navy blue roll-neck jumper and pale blue jeans and her heart, as always, skipped its customary beat when she first caught sight of him. Once he'd satisfied himself that she really was feeling better he wasted no time in coming to the point.

'Why didn't you tell me?' he asked quietly.

'I hadn't known very long myself,' she replied cautiously, skirting his question.

'But long enough.' He paused. 'So when were you going to tell me—if I hadn't found out in the dramatic way I did?'

'I don't know,' she replied. 'I'm not sure.'

'I take it you were going to tell me?' He stared at her.

'If I hadn't, I guess you soon would have found out,' she replied lightly, 'as we work together.'

'So you weren't considering a termination?' He almost seemed to hold his breath as he waited for her answer.

'No.' She shook her head. 'No, of course not.'

'Ah.' The relief on his face was only too obvious but it was swiftly replaced by a puzzled frown. 'So, once you'd intended to go ahead with the pregnancy, was I to play any role in the baby's future?'

'That rather depended on you and your reaction,' she said.

'And that would rather depend on when you chose to tell me,' he replied swiftly.

'I would have told you,' she said at last, looking levelly at him. 'I just wasn't sure quite when, that's all.'

'I don't quite understand why you felt you had to wait,' he said, shaking his head.

'I didn't know what your reaction would be.'

'You thought I might be upset?'

'Well, aren't you?'

'Why would I be?'

'Well, this is hardly a conventional situation. I mean, you and I aren't exactly in a stable relationship, one in which a pregnancy would be received with delight, are we? I imagine,' she went on, not giving him time to answer, 'that you were as shocked by this news as I was.'

'Well, yes,' he agreed, 'I suppose I was. It could only have happened during that weekend we spent together and I'd thought the precautions we'd taken had been adequate. Obviously I was wrong. On the other hand, no contraception is ever one hundred per cent,'

'So you never doubted the baby is yours,' she said quietly.

'What?' He stared at her then shook his head and said, 'No. No, of course not.' When she remained silent he lowered his head in order to be able to look into her face. 'Chrissie, you're not trying to tell me something, are you?'

'Like what?' She looked up raising her eyebrows.

'I don't know—like the baby isn't mine or something?'

'No, Sean.' She shook her head. 'Nothing like that. Of course the baby is yours.'

He made a sound, an exhalation of breath, which could have meant anything from relief to resignation or even satisfaction. Suddenly Chrissie wished he would hold her, hold her close and tell her he loved her, that she and the coming baby meant more to him than anything else in the world, but somehow she doubted that anything of that magnitude was very likely.

'So why were you so wary about my reaction to the news?' he asked after a moment.

'I just couldn't see a baby fitting into your plans or your lifestyle,' she replied lightly.

'Well, certainly a baby didn't exactly feature on my immediate agenda,' he said with a laugh, 'but, well, agendas sometimes have to be amended to fit the circumstances, don't they?'

'I guess so.' She gave a little shrug.

'I can't imagine a baby featured in your plans either,' he said after a moment.

'I always felt I wanted children one day.'

'But not yet.'

'But not yet,' she agreed. 'I was hoping to move my career along before that, although there doesn't seem to be much chance of that now—but, like you say, unexpected things happen and we have to be prepared to adapt.'

'And take responsibility,' he added, and at his words her heart sank. That was what all this was about—Sean taking responsibility for his actions, nothing at all to do with loving her or wanting her for herself.

'You will let me be involved, Chrissie?' he said urgently. As he spoke he leaned forward in his chair so that his face was only a few inches away from hers. If she leaned forward just fractionally, she could have touched his lips with her own. But that would have been madness because this wasn't about that, just as when he had first come over from Ireland it had been nothing to do with her. This also was about the baby and not about her.

'Chrissie,' he said softly, urgently, 'do you think there's a chance we could make a go of things?'

'Because of the baby, you mean?' she whispered.

'Well, yes, of course because of the baby,' he said, 'but not only that.' But Chrissie had stood up abruptly and turned away from him.

'I have a lot of thinking to do, Sean,' she said, 'but right now I'm not sure I'm up to that.'

'No,' he said briskly and stood up. 'Neither should you even try. You still need to rest, which is why I'm going to fix a meal for us both.'

'A meal?' she said weakly.

'Don't look so surprised,' he said with a laugh. 'I'll have you know I have a reputation for my Spanish omelette.'

'In that case, who am I to argue?' she said.

He was true to his word and as they lingered over the meal, which proved to be delicious, Chrissie once again found herself wishing fervently that things could have been different between them, that Sean was the type who wanted to settle down and that he could love her for herself.

After their meal he brewed fresh coffee and while they were drinking it he suddenly clapped his hand to his forehead as if he'd just remembered something.

'What is it?' Startled she looked up.

'I almost forgot,' he said. 'Liam Flynn.'

'What about him?'

'He's here.'

She stared at him. 'What do you mean, he's here?'

'What I said. He's here in Franchester. He turned up at my flat just before I came over here.'

'But what did he want? Does Alison know?' she added before he could answer.

'Well, I would think she does by now,' he said, glancing at his wristwatch. 'He was going to meet her when she came off her shift.'

'Well I hope he isn't going to upset her again,' declared Chrissie. 'I felt just lately she might have started to get over him.'

'Are you saying she really cared for him?'

'Yes, of course she did. She was gutted when he didn't contact her.'

'Well, apparently he's here because he couldn't get Alison out of his mind.'

'I don't believe it!' Chrissie gaped at him in astonishment.

'How do you think she'll take it?' asked Sean.

'Oh, I think she'll be over the moon,' said Chrissie.

'Lucky old Liam.' Sean stood up.

'Where are you going?' she demanded.

'Home,' he said, 'to let you get some rest.'

'I'm perfectly all right,' she protested.

'Fine, but I'm not going to be the one who has to ex-

plain to Tom Fielding if you suffer any ill effects through
not getting enough rest.'

'Sean, it's Caitlin.'

'Hello, Cait.' The call came through from his sister-in-
law just as he returned to his flat.

'How is Chrissie?' she asked.

'She's doing well. She's home and I've just been to
see her.'

'And I take it that everything is fine with the baby?'

'Tom Fielding says so.'

'Well, that's wonderful.' The pleasure was obvious in
Caitlin's voice. 'Michael and I are banking on a happy-
ever-after ending here, Sean.'

'It might be a bit early days to be thinking on those
lines,' he said cautiously.

'I don't see why,' she protested. 'Surely now with a baby
on the way…' She trailed off but before he had the chance
to say anything she said, 'You do love Chrissie, don't you?'

'Of course I do. You know I do.'

'But does Chrissie know that?'

'What do you mean?' He frowned.

'Well, have you actually told her how much you love
her?'

'Of course… At least, maybe not in so many words…
but…'

'Honestly!' There was exasperation in Caitlin's tone
now. 'You O'Reagan men are both the same—full of charm
and blarney but curiously reticent when it actually comes
to saying those all-important three little words. For goodness' sake, tell her, Sean, tell her how much you love her.
It will be exactly what she wants to hear, especially now.'

'Well, I was going to tell her...' He trailed off. 'You don't think it will be rushing her too much?'

'No, of course not.'

'You warned me about that before, Caitlin—not rushing her.'

'I know I did, but then I wasn't too sure of your feelings and I didn't want to see Chrissie get hurt again—she suffered dreadfully last time. But now I know how you feel, and I really don't think you should waste any more time.' She paused. 'Oh, by the way, Sean, one other thing—did you know that Liam is here?'

'Yes, I've seen him. I pointed him in Alison's direction. I hope I did the right thing.'

'I would say you did exactly the right thing,' Caitlin replied.

'So at least I've got something right,' said Sean with a rueful laugh.

'All you need to do now is put everything right,' Caitlin responded.

It was late afternoon and Chrissie had just woken from a nap when she heard her doorbell ring. When she went downstairs to answer the door it was to find Alison on the step—a radiant, bright-eyed Alison.

'Oh, Chrissie.' She hugged her friend ecstatically. 'Have you heard?'

'Yes, Alison, I've heard. Sean told me and I'm so, so happy for you. But don't let's stand about here. Come upstairs.'

'I hope I didn't wake you,' said Alison breathlessly as she followed Chrissie up the stairs, 'but I couldn't wait— I just had to come and see you.'

'I'm surprised you could drag yourself away so soon,' said Chrissie with a chuckle, leading the way into her sitting room.

'We've been together all afternoon and he's gone to see Caitlin and Michael. They'd offered to let him stay with them while he's here but, well, there's no need for that.'

'Alison...you're not rushing in again, are you?' said Chrissie warningly.

'No, I don't think so—it's the real thing this time, Chrissie I just know it is. And he knows it is as well. He's come all this way just to see me because he was missing me so much—just like Sean did with you.'

'Well, not quite,' said Chrissie dryly. 'We all know why Sean came to England, and it wasn't just to see me.'

'Actually, Chrissie,' said Alison turning to face her, 'you're wrong there, quite wrong, and that's what I've come to tell you.'

'What do you mean?' Chrissie frowned.

'Well, you always thought that Sean came to England purely because of his interview, then when he got the job he made arrangements to move here—didn't you?'

'Well, yes, that's right.'

'Not entirely,' said Alison. The expression on her face reminded Chrissie of that of a conjurer who was about to pull a rabbit out of a hat. 'Liam has just told me,' Alison went on triumphantly, 'that Sean had made up his mind to move to England even if he didn't get the registrar's job.'

'So?' Chrissie shrugged. 'Maybe he thought he'd stand a better chance here of furthering his career.'

'That apparently wasn't the reason,' said Alison. 'Liam said that Sean told him that he was coming to England because of you, and that even before he came for the interview he'd handed in his notice at St Luke's in Dublin.'

As Alison's words sank in she stared at her friend in amazement. 'I think you've misjudged him, Chrissie,' said Alison quietly at last. 'I think he really loves you and has done so from the moment he set eyes on you.'

'But he said he wasn't the type to settle down,' protested Chrissie shakily.

'People change, Chrissie, you know that, and I think from that weekend in Ireland, after meeting you, Sean changed and came to realise exactly what it was he really wanted. And now there's a baby on the way.'

'I don't want him to think I've trapped him…' Chrissie began hesitantly.

'Trapped him?' Alison almost exploded. 'Far from it. I would say for Sean that will simply complete his happiness.'

'Do you think so, Alison?' said Chrissie fighting to hold back sudden tears. 'Do you really think so?'

'Yes, Chrissie, I do,' Alison replied firmly, 'but what happens now really is down to you.'

After Alison had gone Chrissie sat in the gathering dusk, thinking over all her friend had told her. If what Liam had said about Sean's reason for coming to England was true, and there was no reason to suppose otherwise, then it put a whole new slant on events. She still couldn't quite understand his reasons for not telling her about the interview, but obviously those reasons had been quite valid to him and maybe he really had thought it might have upset her had she known they had been in competition with each other. She hadn't believed him when he'd said he hadn't thought he'd had a chance of getting the job, that he'd thought it would go to an insider, but now, in the light of Liam's remarks, it seemed that he really hadn't been too sure or even too bothered about the job. And that if he hadn't got it he would have simply looked for another in the same area because it meant being near her.

She'd been angry with him, horribly angry, imagining he'd used her, when all the time it now seemed that wonderful weekend they had shared had been for real. Since then she had insisted their relationship be professional, had been cool and distant with him, until that night at the club which had proved to her there was still chemistry between them. And then with the discovery of her pregnancy she had been terrified he would think she had trapped him into doing the decent thing or, even worse, that he would do the decent thing purely for the baby and not for her.

Now it seemed she'd been wrong all along. Now, as Alison had said, it was down to her to put things right. With a hand that shook slightly, she picked up the phone.

It was dark by the time Sean arrived and Chrissie had lit two lamps in her sitting room, together with a candle, which she set on the coffee-table. Its scent permeated the room with a light floral fragrance. When he rang the doorbell she went downstairs to let him in, then wordlessly led him up to her flat where at last she turned to face him.

'Thank you for coming over,' she said, desperately trying to ignore the racing of her pulse.

'I was going to come anyway,' he said softly. Reaching out, he gently brushed the side of her cheek with the backs of his fingers.

'Were you?' she said in surprise. 'You were only here this afternoon.'

'I know, but there was something I wanted to tell you—something I should have told you a long time ago.'

'Oh,' she said, thrown suddenly by the look in his eyes.

'But you go first,' he said. 'Why did you want to see me?'

'I wanted to say I was sorry,' she said.

'Whatever for?' It was his turn to look surprised.

'For thinking that you'd only come to England for your interview. Liam told Alison that you'd planned to come here whether you got the job at Ellie's or not.'

'And did he tell her why?'

'He said it was because you wanted to be with me,' she said.

'I tried to tell you that,' he said ruefully.

'I know you did,' she replied, 'and I didn't believe you, and when you got here and we spent that weekend together I thought you'd just used the situation. I know now I was wrong, and that's why I'm trying to tell you I'm sorry. I should never have doubted you, Sean.' Her voice shook as she spoke and he stepped forward and drew her into his arms. It felt good to be there again and gratefully she leaned against him.

'It's understandable that you were wary,' he said after a moment, 'after the way Alan Peterson treated you. And let's face it, Chrissie, my own track record has been pretty colourful. But do you know something? Almost from the moment I met you, I knew you were the woman I wanted to be with for the rest of my life.'

'And yet you told me at the wedding that the last thing you wanted was to settle down, like Michael and Caitlin.'

'I know I did,' he admitted, 'but I'd barely even spoken to you then. But gradually as I got to know you something happened to me. Michael told me it would happen that way—that the only reason I didn't think I ever wanted to settle down was because I hadn't met the right woman. He also said that when it happened I would know, and he was absolutely right. I love you, Chrissie, that's what I was coming here to tell you tonight. If I'm honest, I think I've loved you from the moment I set eyes on you.'

'I love you, too,' she whispered, 'and I'm sorry I doubted you.' As she spoke she lifted her hands, cupped his face and drew it down to hers, her lips parting in welcome. His kiss was warm and exciting, so exciting that after a long while wrapped in each other's arms they had to remind themselves that Chrissie was still suffering from the effects of the accident and a threatened miscarriage.

'How do you really feel about the baby?' she asked him when they finally drew apart and they sat close together on the sofa, Sean's arm around her shoulders as she snuggled against him.

'Amazed—shocked, even,' he said. 'Apprehensive that we will have a new life to care for, but at the same time over the moon. What about you?' He glanced down at her.

'The same, really. But do you know what I was afraid of?'

'No, tell me.'

'I was afraid that once you knew about the baby you would feel you had to do the decent thing and marry me— not because you wanted to, because you wanted me, but for the baby's sake. I was so afraid you would think that I had trapped you.'

'Oh, my love, I would never think that.' Putting his hand beneath her chin, he tilted it and kissed the tip of her nose. 'I am overjoyed that we are to have a baby and when you were in hospital and there was a chance that you might miscarry, I was devastated. And as for you thinking I would simply be staying with you for the baby's sake—well, all I can tell you is that I knew I wanted to marry you long before I knew about the baby.' He broke off as if a sudden thought had hit him. 'You *will* marry me, won't you, Chrissie?' he added urgently.

'Oh, Sean, yes, of course I will…'

'Before the baby is born?'

'Yes, of course before the baby is born. And from now on, my darling, we tell each other everything—no more secrets.'

'No more secrets,' he agreed. They were silent for a long moment as each of them reflected on the past and all that had happened between them.

'Do you know what I'd really like?' It was Chrissie who at last broke the silence.

'No, darling,' Sean replied looking tenderly down at her as she nestled against his shoulder. 'You tell me and if I can make it happen, I will.'

'I would like us to be married in Ireland,' she said, 'at the same church as Michael and Caitlin, and to have the reception at Ballinsale Castle. I would like all our friends to be there, including Alison and Liam, of course, and Pat and Noreen from the pub…' She paused. 'Noreen knew, didn't she? About us, I mean.'

'Yes, she did,' Sean agreed, 'and I don't see any reason why we can't do as you want, although there's only one thing I might not be able to arrange.'

'Oh?' she said looking up at him. 'And what's that?'

'The snow,' he said. 'I doubt I can arrange any snow.'

'I think,' she said, lifting her face once more for his kiss, 'that under the circumstances I might just be able to forgo the snow.'

MILLS & BOON®

Live the emotion

JANUARY 2006 HARDBACK TITLES

ROMANCE™

The Italian Duke's Wife *Penny Jordan*	H6308	0 263 19102 8
Shackled by Diamonds *Julia James*	H6309	0 263 19103 6
Bought by her Husband *Sharon Kendrick*	H6310	0 263 19104 4
The Royal Marriage *Fiona Hood-Stewart*	H6311	0 263 19105 2
The Desert Virgin *Sandra Marton*	H6312	0 263 19106 0
At the Cattleman's Command *Lindsay Armstrong*		
	H6313	0 263 19107 9
The Millionaire's Runaway Bride *Catherine George*		
	H6314	0 263 19108 7
His Secretary Mistress *Chantelle Shaw*	H6315	0 263 19109 5
The Wedding Arrangement *Lucy Gordon*	H6316	0 263 19110 9
His Inherited Wife *Barbara McMahon*	H6317	0 263 19111 7
Marriage Reunited *Jessica Hart*	H6318	0 263 19112 5
O'Reilly's Bride *Trish Wylie*	H6319	0 263 19113 3
Counterfeit Princess *Raye Morgan*	H6320	0 263 19114 1
Newborn Daddy *Judy Christenberry*	H6321	0 263 19115 X
High-Altitude Doctor *Sarah Morgan*	H6322	0 263 19116 8
The Surgeon's Pregnancy Surprise *Laura MacDonald*		
	H6323	0 263 19117 6

HISTORICAL ROMANCE™

The Enigmatic Rake *Anne O'Brien*	H621	0 263 19030 7
The Silver Lord *Miranda Jarrett*	H622	0 263 19031 5
His Duty, Her Destiny *Juliet Landon*	H623	0 263 19032 3

MEDICAL ROMANCE™

His Secret Love-Child *Marion Lennox*	M533	0 263 19078 1
Her Honourable Playboy *Kate Hardy*	M534	0 263 19079 X

MILLS & BOON®

Live the emotion

JANUARY 2006 LARGE PRINT TITLES

ROMANCE™

The Ramirez Bride *Emma Darcy*	1831	0 263 18923 6
Exposed: The Sheikh's Mistress *Sharon Kendrick*		
	1832	0 263 18924 4
The Sicilian Marriage *Sandra Marton*	1833	0 263 18925 2
At the French Baron's Bidding *Fiona Hood-Stewart*		
	1834	0 263 18926 0
Their New-Found Family *Rebecca Winters*	1835	0 263 18927 9
The Billionaire's Bride *Jackie Braun*	1836	0 263 18928 7
Contracted: Corporate Wife *Jessica Hart*	1837	0 263 18929 5
Impossibly Pregnant *Nicola Marsh*	1838	0 263 18930 9

HISTORICAL ROMANCE™

Betrayed and Betrothed *Anne Ashley*	319	0 263 18899 X
The Abducted Heiress *Claire Thornton*	320	0 263 18900 7
Marrying Miss Hemingford *Mary Nichols*	321	0 263 19066 8

MEDICAL ROMANCE™

The Celebrity Doctor's Proposal *Sarah Morgan*		
	589	0 263 18851 5
Undercover at City Hospital *Carol Marinelli*	590	0 263 18852 3
A Mother for His Family *Alison Roberts*	591	0 263 18853 1
A Special Kind of Caring *Jennifer Taylor*		
	592	0 263 18854 X

1205 Gen Std LP

MILLS & BOON®

Live the emotion

FEBRUARY 2006 HARDBACK TITLES

ROMANCE™

The Billionaire Boss's Forbidden Mistress *Miranda Lee*
H6324 0 263 19118 4
Million-Dollar Love-Child *Sarah Morgan*   H6325 0 263 19119 2
The Italian's Forced Bride *Kate Walker*   H6326 0 263 19120 6
The Greek's Bridal Purchase *Susan Stephens*
H6327 0 263 19121 4
The Wedlocked Wife *Maggie Cox*   H6328 0 263 19122 2
At the Spaniard's Convenience *Margaret Mayo*
H6329 0 263 19123 0
The Antonides Marriage Deal *Anne Mcallister* H6330 0 263 19124 9
In The Sheikh's Arms *Sue Swift*   H6331 0 263 19125 7
Meant-To-Be Marriage *Rebecca Winters*   H6332 0 263 19126 5
The Five-Year Baby Secret *Liz Fielding*   H6333 0 263 19127 3
Blue Moon Bride *Renee Roszel*   H6334 0 263 19128 1
Millionaire Dad: Wife Needed *Natasha Oakley*
H6335 0 263 19129 X
Baby on Board *Susan Meier*   H6336 0 263 19130 3
Falling for the Sheikh *Carol Grace*   H6337 0 263 19131 1
A Knight to Hold on to *Lucy Clark*   H6338 0 263 19132 X
Her Boss and Protector *Joanna Neil*   H6339 0 263 19133 8

HISTORICAL ROMANCE™

A Promise To Return *Gail Whitiker*   H624   0 263 19033 1
The Golden Lord *Miranda Jarrett*   H625   0 263 19034 X
His Rebel Bride *Helen Dickson*   H626   0 263 19035 8

MEDICAL ROMANCE™

The Doctor's Unexpected Proposal *Alison Roberts*
M535   0 263 19080 3
The Doctor's Surprise Bride *Fiona McArthur*
M536   0 263 19081 1

MILLS & BOON®

Live the emotion

FEBRUARY 2006 LARGE PRINT TITLES

ROMANCE™

The Brazilian's Blackmailed Bride *Michelle Reid*
1839 0 263 18931 7
Expecting the Playboy's Heir *Penny Jordan*
1840 0 263 18932 5
The Tycoon'sTrophy Wife *Miranda Lee*   1841 0 263 18933 3
Wedding Vow of Revenge *Lucy Monroe*
1842 0 263 18934 1
Marriage at Murraree *Margaret Way*   1843 0 263 18935 X
Winning Back His Wife *Barbara McMahon* 1844 0 263 18936 8
Just Friends To...Just Married *Renee Roszel*
1845 0 263 18937 3
The Shock Engagement *Ally Blake*   1846 0 263 18938 4

HISTORICAL ROMANCE™

The Marriage Debt *Louise Allen*   322 0 263 18801 5
The Rake and the Rebel *Mary Brendan*   323 0 263 18802 3
The Engagement *Kate Bridges*   324 0 263 19067 6

MEDICAL ROMANCE™

Holding Out for a Hero *Caroline Anderson*   593 0 263 18855 8
His Unexpected Child *Josie Metcalfe*   594 0 263 18856 6
A Family Worth Waiting For *Margaret Barker*
595 0 263 18857 4
Where the Heart Is *Kate Hardy*   596 0 263 18858 2

0106 Gen Std LP